Interludes

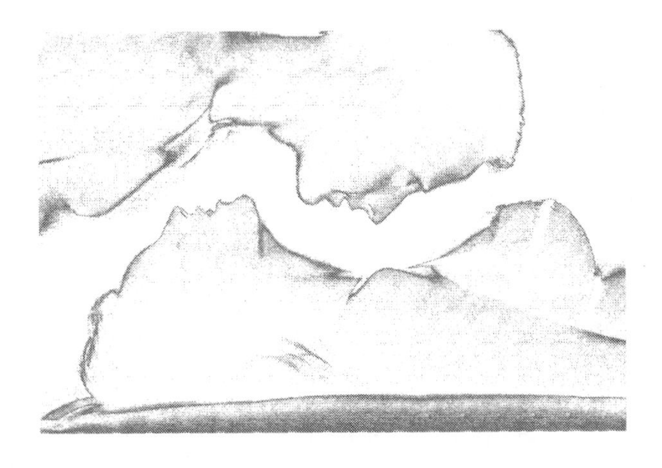

by Harmony Kent

Interludes

By Harmony Kent

ISBN: 1530002648
ISBN-13: 978-1530002641

Hello, and thank you for purchasing Interludes. In writing this short story collection, I wanted to not only enter new waters (for me) in producing erotic romantic fiction, but also to stretch myself further (ahem) by setting specific word limits for each tale. With this in mind, I allocated a set word count for each chapter. 1000 for chapter 1, 2000 for chapter 2, 3000 for chapter 3, and so on up to 10,000 for chapter 10.

I would love to know what you think of the resulting book—what you weren't so keen on as well as what you loved, and what you might like to see more of from me.

You can contact me via my website at http://harmonykent.co.uk. And I would love it if you felt moved enough to leave me a book review on Amazon and Goodreads.

To hear about my newest releases, sign up for my mailing list at http://eepurl.com/bQ0qwX.

A collection of short erotic fiction that will tickle more than your taste buds and wet more than your appetite.

With a range of genres and styles, this book has enough steam for everyone.

GREY MANCHESTER—contemporary romance in 1000 words. Will Nadine choose to drop her knife or her knickers?

DOUBLE TROUBLE—ménage à trois in 2000 words. After a dry spell, Sophia gets more than she bargained for with a solicitor and a teacher.

DRAGON KISSED—shifter romance in 3000 words. Jenna's life is fairly run of the mill until she has a flying accident. With a dragon. All is not as it seems in this fiery romance.

TRYST—contemporary romance in 4000 words. Polly pushes the boundaries on a workplace night out.

LOVE ON THE CORNISH LINE—contemporary romance in 5000 words. Becky falls flat on her face, and madly in love. Her weekly commute home proves to be anything but routine.

THE INLAW—contemporary romance in 6000 words. At 43, amputee Carla never expected in her wildest dreams to be called a MILF by a hot young stud. Trouble is, he's her son in law's brother. And young enough to be her son. Sparks fly when she's caught with her hands in the biscuit tin.

NIGHT NURSE—contemporary romance in 7000

words. Denise has only weeks left to live. What constitutes life, though? What fills the yawning hours of empty days? Who are you once the chemo and the cancer have stripped you bare? What to do?—Go out on a slow fizzle, or with a big bang?

OVERBOARD—contemporary romance in 8000 words. When Stella falls overboard in the middle of the Pacific, she gets more than she bargained for. Sharks and storms not withstanding.

ALIEN LIAISON—alien romance in 9000 words. When the military transport, Lunas Two, crash lands on Zorth, Jay is given the job of liaising with the locals. She's seen plenty of aliens in her four years of service, but never one as finger licking good as Lemo. How far will she have to go to keep the peace?

SAVING FACE—historical romance in 10,000 words. Non-related step brother and sister, David and Annalise, break all the rules in this steamy historical romance. Forced to live apart from the love of her life and into an arranged and loveless marriage, Annalise has to grow up fast. When all is lost, will she be able to save face?

READER ADVISORY: This book contains explicit sex scenes and language hot enough to burn your pages. For mature readers only.

Contents Page

Chapter One—Grey Manchester 1
Chapter Two—Double Trouble 6
Chapter Three—Dragonkissed 14
Chapter Four—Tryst 25
Chapter Five—Love on the Cornish Line 38
Chapter Six—The Inlaw 54
Chapter Seven—Night Nurse 72
Chapter Eight—Overboard 92
Chapter Nine—Alien Liaison 115
Chapter Ten—Saving Face 139
More Books from the Author 168

CHAPTER ONE

Grey Manchester

Nadine Sparrow looked at the knife in her hands. Then her glance drifted through the window. Hailstone bounced on the crowded rooftops. Manchester—grey, noisy—a place that encouraged her irritability. Then she saw something in the distance, or rather, some*one*. The figure of Andrew Parker strode down the road. Full of purpose. Oh dear. Nadine gripped the knife and swallowed.

When Andrew's tall figure drew near, his cruel sneer came into awful focus. She glanced at her reflection in the glass. Skinny, brunette, and not pretty. The faded, yellowing bruise didn't help her appearance any. Lord, but she needed a G & T. Or, perhaps a whisky, early in the day as it was. This terrible weather made it feel a lot later, though. Even at two in the afternoon, she needed the lights on.

The hail sounded like hundreds of mice skittering across the roof tiles, making Nadine cross. With the back of the knife-hand, she rubbed at the dull ache that had settled in her forehead.

What did he want? With a sigh, Nadine went to meet him.

Due to the heavy, unrelenting hail, she waited in the doorway while he made his way down the short garden path. He stopped at the bottom of the low doorstep and looked up at her. His eyes glinted.

They stared at one another through lonely, hurt eyes. Could she cope with this today? What did he have in store for her? Nadine regarded Andrew's plump, pink lips. Absently, she fingered the knife.

'You'd better come in, I suppose.' She took care to shape the words on her lips for him.

He nodded and followed her down the hallway and into the kitchen.

She wanted to turn her back on him, stare out the window, something, anything, to avoid having to look at him. That wouldn't work, though. With a sigh, she leant against the old wooden worktop instead.

He stared at her for a moment, and then raised his hands. Ambivalent, torn between two kinds of passion—the angry kind and the aroused kind—she watched while he formed the signs he needed.

You owe me, he said.

Nadine shook her head. 'I don't have the funds.'

He sighed, looked at the floor for a full five seconds, and then captured her gaze. *Look, I hate this—us—I want* ... He raised his hands in the air in a helpless gesture.

'What do you want?' Nadine asked. The metal handle of the knife felt hot in her hand. Why hadn't she put it down yet? What did she intend? Which kind of payment would she give him?

They returned to their silent stare-off, and Nadine felt even more ambivalent toward this man who had been her friend since primary school. As a precocious five-year-old, his deafness had intrigued her and drawn her to him. She'd learned sign language for him, and how to lip-speak. Today, she deliberately withheld signing. Make him work for her words.

She hated that they couldn't yell and scream at one another when they needed to blow off steam. Well, she could yell at him, but his deaf-muteness always rendered her thunder pointless and ineffectual.

Frustration ... such an apt word. It described a multitude of feelings and unfulfilled want.

Noisy thoughts tore the taut silence asunder. Could she, in all fairness, continue to blame him for the attack? One punch—that's all. Self-defence. He hadn't heard her approach. She ought to have known better. His recent assault had left him jittery and vulnerable.

Nadine stared at his delicate hands, now clenched while his arms hung at his sides. She loved those hands. Those flexible fingers. The things they could do to her. A memory grew wings and fluttered in front of her. Their first time. His touch. The first time he'd touched her in *that way.* Two not-quite-sixteen-year-olds discovering each other. Discovering sex. Love.

She took a step forward, knife still gripped within sweaty fingers. Her pulse raced. 'I lied. I do have the funds.'

His eyes widened in question.

'Here's what I owe you.'

She took another step toward him. Stopped. Sidestepped so that the low wooden table stood immediately behind her. Eyes locked on his, Nadine reached behind her and placed the knife on the rough wooden surface. Then she reached down to the knee-length hem of her skirt and pulled it up to her waist, baring her lacy panties.

Andrew stared, surprised and blushing. He glanced up at her.

'Come and get it,' she said with a smile.

I'm sorry, he signed.

At last. That's all she'd needed—an apology. Why had it taken him so long? She studied his expression. Looked at what she'd taken as a sneer while he walked down the footpath. Her annoyance evaporated. He wasn't a cruel man. Just proud and ashamed. And trying to make amends.

Nadine waved a hand to drag his attention from her crotch to her face. 'Why did you start by going on about the money I owe you?'

He shrugged. Blushed some more. *I needed an excuse to come and see you.* He grinned and shook his head. Took a hesitant step her way. *I'm sorry.*

For reply, Nadine slipped off her underwear. Slid up onto the table. Beckoned him forward.

His blush deepened, but no longer with embarrassment. He came to her.

Nadine took hold of his waistband and pulled him in close. Hungry hands fumbled with his zip. Freed, his manhood stood at attention. Wet and ready and too impatient for foreplay, she manoeuvred until he lay at her slick entrance. In one smooth jerk, he thrust into her.

She gripped his hips and rocked with him. He set a hard, fast pace. Nadine arched her spine, threw back her head, and moaned with pleasure. He'd never fucked her before. It had always been slow and gentle—making love.

The skittering mice accompanied her screams as she came.

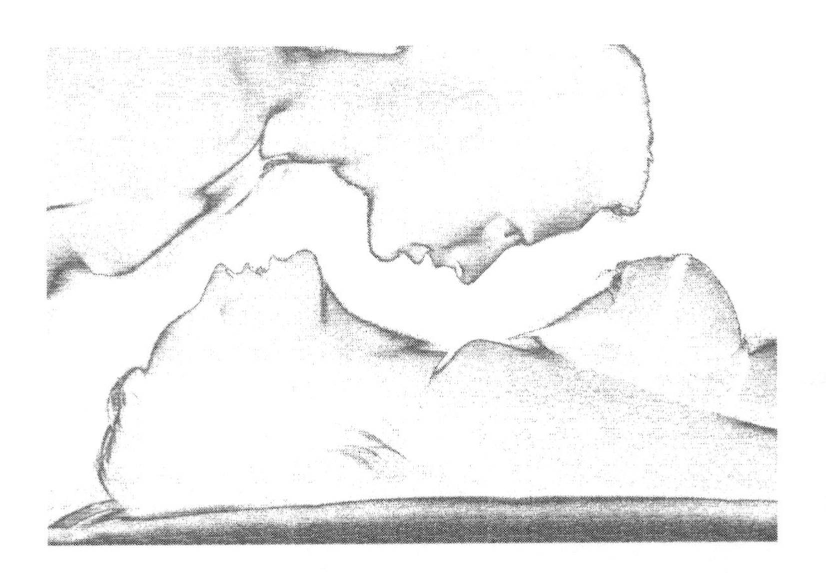

CHAPTER TWO

Double Trouble

Dr Sophia Cockle flipped off the light on the x-ray viewer and turned to her patient. The old man gave her a hopeful smile. She perched on the edge of a hard plastic chair and leant toward him. 'Mr Dennis? Good news.'

'Aye?'

'Yes.' She smiled. 'It's not broken. Just a sprain. I'll have a nurse strap it up for you, and you can be on your way.'

'Oh, thank you, Doctor.'

Sophia rose, gave the man a final smile, then turned and left the exam cubicle. A scan around A & E showed her that she had no pressing duties just now. At three on a Wednesday morning, the place stood nearly deserted. Her weekend shift would be a different story entirely. Might as well enjoy it while she could.

Coffee in hand, Sophia sank into one of the old faux-leather chairs in the break room and slipped her phone from her pocket. A thumb-swipe brought the screen to life. No calls. A dismayed sigh escaped her lips.

Until she'd met sexy, thin, Christian Sweet—a solicitor with a passion for books—her life had been going nowhere. After allowing her best friend to set her up on a blind date, Sophia believed she'd found *the one.* Well, perhaps not. Why hadn't he called? Had she gone too far?

Divorced at forty-five with a twenty-five-year-old son who'd only just left home, Sophia's dating experience was limited. What was acceptable these days? She hadn't planned to have sex with the man. But—oh goodness—it'd been as hot as him.

Girl Town flooded just thinking about it. Parked in the bowels of a multi-storey car park, hidden in shadows, she'd gone down on him. Taken his thick length into her small mouth. Then he'd taken care of her. In the car. In a goddam car park, for crying out loud. And she had. Many times. He'd finger-fucked her, both front and back at the same time—a first. They'd ended up at his place, and rode all night.

A week, now, without a call. Not so much as a text. Sophia felt determined that she wouldn't be the one to cave and call him. As Emma, her BFF, loved to say: no shortage of burger to go with her fries. Which would be true, if she'd settle for fast food. However, she wanted the whole three-course meal, complete with candlelight and romance. At her age, she should know better.

Disgruntled, she dropped the offending mobile into her pocket and sipped at her Cappuccino. A couple of minutes' peace, and then Sister poked her head through the doorway. Sophia raised her eyebrows in question.

Becca grinned. 'Live one for you. Cubicle three. RTA. Possible dislocated shoulder.'

'Okay. Be there in two.'

Becca gave a last smile and disappeared. Sophia sighed and eased to her feet, half-full-paper-cup of coffee in hand, and made her way to the medical station in Minors. As she set her drink down, she glanced across the large open space toward Majors. They seemed just as quiet tonight. File in hand, Sophia strolled over to cubicle three and pulled the curtain back.

Then she pulled up short. An Adonis of a man reclined on the exam bench, his baby-blues fixed on her as she stood there, gawping. It took a lot of effort to move her feet and walk into the small space. Even more application to hold out her hand and shake his.

'Mr …' She glanced at the file. 'Mr Greenaway. I'm Dr Cockle. What seems to be the trouble?'

He looked somewhat sheepish when he replied, 'I had an argument with a lamppost.'

Sophia grinned and nodded. 'No doubt the ice had a hand in it?'

He returned the grin and the nod, then winced and raised his good hand to his misshapen shoulder. Sophia put the file down and leant over him. 'Let me take a look?'

He lay back and nodded again. With gentle fingers, she eased open his shirt and examined him. A definite dislocation, but she would have to send him to X-ray before manipulating it. Also, it being an RTA, she needed to do neuro obs too, as well as a general check over. Well, it would pass the time, and he wasn't exactly hard on the eyes.

On Thursday, Sophia sat in the bar and waited, a little nervous. Why had she agreed to meet him? Roy Greenaway had turned out to be entertaining and easygoing. A school teacher by trade, he had no right to sport such ripped abs. It should be illegal. She shook her head and smiled. Of course, Emma had been all for this little tête à tête.

A nervous sip of Chardonnay later, and the door opened. Along with the blast of icy air, in came Adonis—er, Roy. Oh boy, Girl Town was seeing plenty of flash floods these days. Sophia clenched her thighs together. No way would she make the same mistake again. No way. Uh uh. So not happening …

The best intentions and all that. Was she having a mid-life or what? Sophia aimed the hot water from the shower head at the soreness between her legs. Roy made a good teacher—he'd taught her a lot last night. Better still, by the time she'd driven home, he'd texted her … twice. She cursed the fact of her nightshift tonight. Between their joint schedules, they wouldn't be able to get together until Monday.

They exchanged messages all weekend, and even indulged in a bit of Sexting. By the time Monday rolled around, Sophia felt as horny as she ever had. Her alarm roused her at one p.m., and as much as she craved coffee, she had to take care of business first. On her back, she slipped a hand into her hot wetness and closed her eyes.

Her fantasy didn't go quite as planned, though. It started out okay, with Roy's face filling her mind's eye. Trouble is, at some point, he morphed into Christian. And then she had the two of them together. A flush of guilt crept up her neck and warmed her cheeks. Then she reprimanded herself, and told herself that it was only a fantasy, after all. It wasn't like she was doing it for real.

All of which would have been fine. A-okay. If *he* hadn't then rang. Why did she take the call? 'Christian. What a surprise.'

'Yeah. Sorry about that. I had this big case I had to work on. It's been mad. I kept meaning to ring, but then I'd get snowed under and, before I knew it, it'd be silly o'clock and too late to call.'

'Right. I see.'

'You thought I wasn't interested?'

Sophia cringed. 'Something like that.'

'I really am sorry. It was thoughtless. Let me make it up to you.'

'No, no. It's fine. Honestly. You don't have to make up for anything—'

'Of course, I do. I behaved like an arsehole. Look, Sophia, I like you. We had a great night, and … well, I want to see you again.'

OMG. She squeezed her eyes shut. Only one thing for it. 'Erm. I sort of went on a date on Thursday.'

'A date?' *(Did you have sex?)* The question within the question hung in the air.

'Yeah. Sorry. I thought, … you know.'

'That I wasn't gonna call.'

'Yeah.' *Shitshitshit.*

Her fantasy, of the two men pleasuring her together, lodged

in the front of her brain and promptly claimed squatter's rights. No shifting that one. What was happening to her? She'd turned into a nymphomaniac. Is that what three years of abstinence did to you? Was it normal?

Sophia cleared her throat. 'I *am* sorry.'

The not-quite-silence of an open line tugged at her guts. Then Christian said, 'So, it's serious then? You like him?'

'Oh. It's—it's early days.' *Why did I say that? He just gave me an out.*

'So, we can have coffee, then? Please. My treat. Give me the chance to make it up to you.'

'Okay, sure.' *Damn traitorous tongue.*

And that's how come she found herself in this untenable situation right now. With this kind of idiocy, it's a miracle she ever finished medical school. Nervous, she flicked her gaze from Christian to Roy and back again. The two men, oblivious to her (for now), stood and stared at one another. If looks could kill. Ho hum.

Words couldn't convey the depths of her self-loathing just then. Unfortunately, no amount of self-flagellation would remedy this travesty. And, really, what were the chances? York was a big city. And this bar nowhere near the hospital or her home—or the school or Roy's flat, for that matter. Christian had taken her to an exclusive wine bar frequented by legal types. What on earth was Roy doing in a place like this?

A chuckle bubbled up and out before she could censor it. After all, it's not like she could blame Roy for being here. The two men broke their visual battle and turned the heat of their furious stares on her. Yeah—perhaps laughing hadn't been the most appropriate (or diplomatic) of responses.

Her attempts at explanation fell on deaf ears. Roy, quite rightly, looked hurt and betrayed. Of course, he did. While Christian looked a tad smug. The git. In the end, she persuaded Roy to sit with them, and then she packed Christian off to get a round in. In his brief absence, she laid it all out for Roy.

He took it in, thought for a while, and then asked, 'Do you like him?'

Sophia chewed on her bottom lip. 'I like you both. And I wasn't going to do anything with him other than meet for a drink. Truly.'

'It's okay. I believe you. I just … I got a shock, is all. And it's not like I have any claim on you.'

'What do you mean?'

God, but this dating thing felt way too complex and complicated.

'Well, we only met the one time …' *And spent the night together.*

'Right.' She chugged back the last of her wine.

Then Christian came back, booze in hand. One drink led to another. And then one thing led to another. Somewhere within all that fuzziness, Sophia confessed her fantasy. Somewhere within all that fuzziness, the three of them ended up at her place. Somewhere within all that fuzziness, make-believe became make-real.

Not that any of them planned it. They started out on her sofa, with more wine, sharing a laugh. Snuggling in. Then hands strayed and lips met.

Sophia lay between the two men. Roy buried his head between her legs while Christian nuzzled her breasts. She'd never felt so erotic in her entire life. Had never done anything like this. By her second orgasm, she wondered why not.

With Roy seated on the sofa, Sophia knelt in front of him and took him into her mouth. Christian took her from behind. An hour later, they moved to the bedroom and her super-kingsized bed.

Fingers and tongues explored, teased, and tantalised. All three gasped and panted while their bodies grew slick. Sophia, wet and hot and aroused as all hell, straddled Christian and slipped down his hard shaft. He groaned and gripped her around her waist. She rocked her hips, and he stilled her. Pulled her forward until she lay on his chest, and her bottom stuck in the air. Behind her, Roy rubbed lubricant around her back passage and toyed with her with his fingers. Then he penetrated her.

Filled front and back felt exquisite. They alternated thrusts and found a delicious rhythm, which soon had Sophia coming.

Over the next weeks and months, they grew into quite the trio. Just when Sophia had thought she'd been condemned to grow old alone, she'd found love with two gorgeous, passionate, and sweet men.

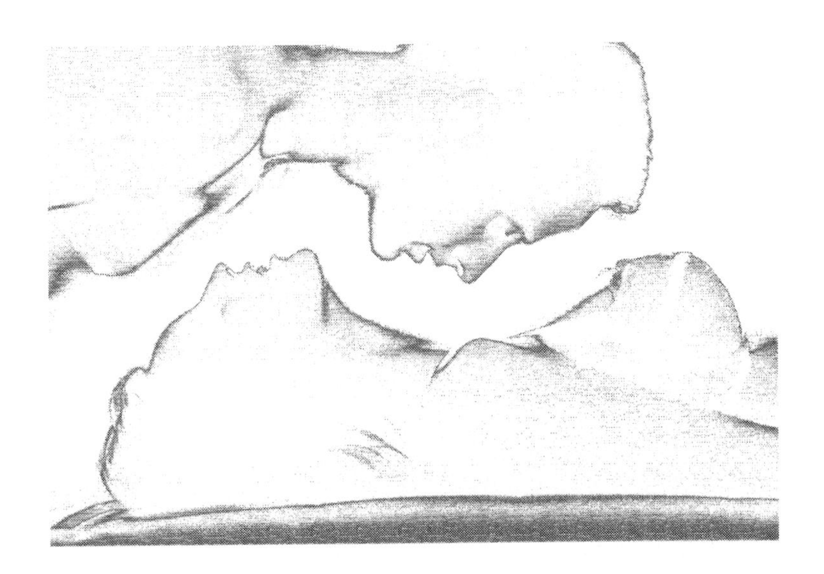

CHAPTER THREE

Dragonkissed

At six years old, Jenna Olsen suspected that something was a little off when her pet lizard spoke to her. Nevertheless, she lived a relatively normal life among other humans.

Until her flying accident. With a dragon.

Hang-gliding had seemed like a great idea. Like fun. Just what she needed, in fact. She took to the air like she'd been born to it. And, for the first time in her life, felt like she belonged.

It (he?) came out of nowhere. Literally out of the blue. One minute, she soared joyfully, riding the thermals. The next, a dark mass blotted out the sun before smacking into her.

Pain roused her. Then snoring. Cold permeated through the back of her thin t-shirt. A foul odour assaulted her nostrils. Heart thumping, Jenna opened her eyes. And blinked. A dragon lay curled up next to her. Fast asleep. What the?

Her whole body throbbed and ached, and the tinny taste of blood coated her tongue. Hard, cold rock prodded and poked into her tender spine. She sat up. Held her breath. The dragon slept on. She was shit out of luck, though, as his recumbent body blocked the only exit she could see from the cave.

Wait. *Cave*? Where the hell was she? A whimper escaped her clamped lips and set jaw. The dragon stirred. Woke.

Jenna tried a smile, which she hoped didn't look like the menacing grimace it felt like. Angry eyes settled on her. She froze. Tensed. More pain stroked her nerves in protest at her contracted muscles.

The dragon watched her for a minute that felt like an hour, and then … *shimmered.* Jenna blinked some more. A man crouched before her. Fuzzy wings poked above his shoulders. Bare shoulders. While she stared, he rose to his feet, in all his naked glory.

Jenna's jaw dropped open. '*Oh.*'

The dragon/man took a couple of steps, but stopped at her breathy exclamation. He watched her some more. The fiery anger bled away from his orbs and revealed dark, chocolate-brown eyes, deep enough for her to drown in. Jenna trembled.

He seemed to reach a decision, and in a single bound, reached her side. He pulled her to her feet and into his chest. His warm chest. His body heat felt like central heating. Her extremities thawed at speed. Jenna wasn't too sure that it wasn't something else helping to warm her, too. The man was hot—in every sense of the term.

Not a word had been spoken yet, which felt just plain weird. Could he speak? A tad calmer now, Jenna eased away from him a little, and straight away missed his comforting warmth. She looked up at him—into those eyes. Her mouth first watered, then dried up. Her heart did an uncomfortable thumpity-thump flutter, and then geared up for a hundred metre sprint.

'Um, hi,' she said. 'My name's Jenna.'

His voice, when it came, washed over her ears like surf over shale. 'Pete. Pete Lakeman.'

'Oh.'

He raised his eyebrows and quirked his lips into a small smile.

'You—you have a name.'

His smile spread all the way into that gorgeous milk chocolate. 'I have a name.'

'Um. … What—what happened?'

His face clouded. 'Yes. I'm sorry about that.' He stared down at her. Jenna stood, ensnared in his gaze. 'I didn't see you until too late. The sun got in my eyes.'

'The sun?' Right. Like a dragon flying through the sky was the most normal thing on the planet. Of course. The sun got in his eyes. Made perfect sense.

He nodded. 'The sun.' Bent his head a fraction toward hers.

Entranced, Jenna tilted her face upward. She could drink his chocolate all day. A hint of that fiery-hue returned to his irises, but it didn't look like anger this time. Jenna's heart sped up even more. If she didn't slow it down soon, it would run away so fast, it would leave her lying in the dust.

In an effort to break the spell and gather her meagre wits, Jenna closed her eyes. And, for some reason, parted her lips a smidgeon. Soft, moist heat covered them. Hot, calloused hands pulled her into his firm chest. Jenna melted into the kiss.

A couple of volcanic eruptions later, he pulled away. A soft moan vied for freedom. Jenna blushed. Molten lava flowed through her veins. 'Oh.'

Her new favourite word. Not the most eloquent, but it held infinite meanings. Covered a multitude of feelings.

Concern stared down at her. 'Are you all right?'

Jenna cleared her throat. Nodded a bit too vigorously. 'Yes. Yes. Fine. Thank you.' Just in case he missed it the first time, she nodded some more.

Get. A. Grip.

His expression clouded. 'I should get you home.'

'Home. Right. Yes.' She nodded again.

A mash-up of emotions flittered across his features—confusion, amusement, desire, annoyance, and … exasperation?

All business, he stepped away from her. With a hard look in his eyes, he told her, 'I shouldn't have kissed you. My apologies.'

Jenna could only stand and stare while her heart stuttered and died. Something cold snaked down through her guts. That look … she repulsed him? Yes. He appeared disgusted.

Great.

Just. Great.

Jenna's words sounded gruff, 'Yes. Please, take me home.'

He stiffened and set his jaw, but nodded. 'I need to shift, and then you have to climb on my back.'

Jenna settled for a single nod. It seemed like the safest bet. Once again, he did the shimmery thing. When he got too bright to focus on, Jenna shut her eyes. Upon opening them, she found the enormous dragon in front of her once more. And that smell … *eew*. With a gulp, she walked toward it. The creature motioned with its head toward its back, as if to say, 'Climb aboard.'

Through the flight home, he remained gracious yet cold and aloof, which stung more than the spiky scales on his back. It came as a big surprise to them both that she could hear his thoughts while in his dragon form. She only wished she'd been able to gain such access while he'd stood in his human guise.

What had changed? Was it something she'd said? Done? She shrugged. She was probably dreaming all this, anyhow. In a coma, maybe. Or dead in a ditch, with her hang-glider scattered in shreds around her. Dragons weren't real.

Right. Like pet lizards didn't talk. Tears kept the memory company. To this day, she missed the little critter like crazy. Not even now, older and supposedly wiser, could she bring herself to forgive her nan. Yes, of course, she could understand the fear it must have given the old lady—to have her young granddaughter insist for months on end that she could talk with her lizard. At first, it had been received with that certain indulgence shared between the very old and the very young. At first. Then had come consternation. And finally, fear. Hot on the heels of that had come anger, and a firm decision.

Jenna had never recovered. Her poor, pet lizard. For the rest of her life, she would remember with desperation the day she'd come home from school to find him gone. Nan never did say what she'd done with him. Then they moved house. Little Jenna had cried for weeks. Inconsolable. Distraught. Unable to trust another soul again. The day Lakey Lizard left her, was the day she left her childhood behind.

Beneath her clamped thighs, the dragon's back changed altitude, and they plummeted earthward. Though filled with trepidation, Jenna welcomed the distraction from her painful thoughts.

Something nibbled at her brain. Tickled it around the edges. Every time she tried to catch it, the phantom dissolved. Only to return the moment she switched her attention.

Curled up on her sofa, brandy in hand, Jenna thought over the day's strange events. When he'd kissed her, it'd felt so right. For the first time in as long as she could remember, her life had seemed to make sense. And she *was* still alive. Sitting here, all these hours later, seemed proof enough of that. It didn't seem to be down to a whack on the head. Still, her universe had shifted. Much like the dragon/man.

Would she see him again?

Well after midnight, with nothing better to do, she dragged herself up to bed. Sleep proved an elusive fiend that night.

The next evening, she dragged herself into work at the local pub—*The Maiden's Arms.* The shift dragged by, and eleven p.m. couldn't come fast enough. Glum and distracted, Jenna turned down the alley that would take her through the play-park and home.

Her feet slowed to a stop as she approached the swings. A sweet old lady sat there, swinging to and fro. Jenna stared. It couldn't be. Her nan smiled. Against rational volition, she took a step forward. Then another. The apparition on the swing—for apparition it must be—beckoned her closer. Motioned for her to claim the swing next to it.

Jenna sank, weak-kneed, onto the small seat. 'You're not my nan. That's just not possible.' She shook her head. Maybe she had given it an almighty whack, after all. Perhaps all of this was down to acute hallucinations. She didn't quite believe that, though, as unbelievable as all this seemed.

The thing that wasn't her nan smiled. Then shifted. It flickered in and out of shadow for a second or two, as though unsure what to settle on. Then it solidified into Mrs Dickens, her English teacher from middle school. A shapeshifter, then. She'd read about them, but hadn't ever imagined they existed.

In an effort to bite down on her fear, Jenna sank her teeth into her tongue. 'What do you want?'

The *thing* smiled. 'To help. Only to help. My sweet. Such a lovely little thing, you are. It doesn't seem right.'

'What doesn't?'

For reply, it pulled a round, spherical object from where a pocket ought to be but wasn't. Jenna stared. A glass globe. A paperweight. It appeared old and weathered, and scratches marred its surface. The thing held it toward her, but Jenna kept her hands to herself.

'What's that?'

'For you. For protection.'

'Protection? From what?'

The thing smiled again and said, 'Beware, sweet maiden fair; for here, dragons be there.'

Jenna gulped. How did it *know?* What was it? Where had it come from? What crazy realm had she been knocked into?

The hand holding the globe waved it around under her nose. 'Take it.'

'Why would I need protection from dragons?'

'Gracious he may be; but darkness, also, shall you see. When into his cups he does sink, he is apt to act when he should stop and think.' It waved the paperweight around some more. 'A weapon you shall require, when a maiden doth the dragon desire.'

Bemused, Jenna stuttered, 'Y-yes, b-but a—a *paperweight?* Seriously?'

Pretend-Mrs-Dickens shook her head and harrumphed. 'Kill the beast, you must. In this globe, you shall trust.'

Enough with the rhyming, already.

The thing shifted again. The globe dropped to the sodden mud with a dull thump. Cinnamon wafted on the air, and brought with it a whiff of rotten eggs. From the dark swirling cloud, a whisper drifted on the breeze, 'Take the weapon. Protect yourself. Watch out for his passion.' As though it had read her mind, it spoke without the rhymes.

Wait. *Had* it read her mind?

It spoke again, 'Remember what they say.'

'Wh-what do they say?'

'Revenge is a dish best served cold.'

With that, the thing vanished, leaving Jenna sitting there alone, trembling. Whatever enchantment had held her there, now lifted. She sprang to her feet and looked around. Aside from the glass globe, nothing out of the ordinary presented itself.

Jenna took a step away, but then stopped. That phantom nibbled at her brain again. With a quick exhale, Jenna bent and retrieved the paperweight. Who knew, it might come in useful, even if she had no clue how or when or why.

The next night, a familiar figure strode into the pub. Pete Lakeman. Adrenaline chased a cocktail of emotions through Jenna's body—fear, pleasure, anticipation, dread. Familiarity wrapped around him like a fondly recalled comfort blanket, and drew Jenna toward him.

Just as the shapeshifter had said, he knocked the beer back as quickly and surely as the clock ticked off the seconds, minutes, and hours. At the end of her shift, he offered to walk her home. Jenna felt conflicted. On the one hand, she wanted to see more of him. Wanted to get to know him better. On the other … but, no; the only thing she'd truly felt afraid of lately was the shapeshifter.

Despite his fuzzy wings and (sometimes) angry eyes, she found herself falling for the dragon/man. Resolved to settle this weirdness once and for all, Jenna nodded her assent, and they departed together.

When they drew near to the swings, Jenna slowed. Pete picked up on her hesitation and paused by her side. 'What is it, little one?'

Her heart stopped. Didn't beat again for a full five seconds. Then her chest squeezed, and she sucked in much-needed air. 'Wh-what did you call me?'

Only Lakey Lizard had ever called her that. At last, at long last, she caught the phantom and shone the light of awareness on it. *The name.* Of course. Pete *Lakeman.* And her lizard—*Lakey.* She turned stunned eyes onto her companion. 'It's you?'

Solemn, he nodded.

The shapeshifter's warning rang in her skull, '*Revenge is a dish best served cold.*' Did he blame her? Did he believe that she'd gotten rid of him? Jenna gasped. Took a step back. Touched the cold glass globe in her pocket.

Could she do it? Kill the only thing she'd ever truly loved? Her mouth worked, but her tongue wouldn't. No words came. She shook her head. This couldn't be happening.

Pete edged closer.

Would he kill her or protect her? What did he intend?

'Talk to me.' His eyes held such care, such love—no way could he mean her harm. Which left only one other option.

After a deep, fortifying breath, Jenna told him of her encounter the previous night. The more she talked, the more his eyes turned fiery and his skin paled.

When she'd done, he nodded. 'Yes. It told you no lie—revenge *is* a dish best served cold. What it didn't mention, was who would partake of the dessert.'

Jenna's hand tightened around the paperweight. 'I don't understand.'

'Let's get you home. We'll walk and talk.' With an uneasy glance, he took in their surroundings, then gripped her elbow and urged her forward.

Turns out that the shapeshifter had a score to settle with the dragon. It also knew of the dragon's feelings for Miss Olsen. His *feelings.*

She knew, now, whom she believed. She pulled the globe from her pocket. Pete froze. Then he lunged.

Jenna yelled and jumped back.

'Drop it. Drop it, now.' His breath came hot on her cheeks as he knocked the offending item out of her hand. It thudded to the ground and rolled away.

In the blink of an eye, he shifted. Fear washed through her. Had she made the right decision? Then he turned his hate-filled glare onto the paperweight. Fire burst from his jaws. He threw the tongue of flame onto the globe and held it there, until nothing remained but molten glass. And then, not even that. The dragon stopped flaming, and then shimmered until Pete stood before her once more. Naked, and all man.

Jenna turned her stricken face to his. 'Wh-what was it?'

'Revenge. That piece of poison would have ended your life.'

'Oh.'

Jenna's knees gave out. Pete scooped her into his arms and swooped her home, where he carried her all the way upstairs and laid her on her bed. He eased down next to her and spooned her from behind. Told her of her history. Her origins. How the dragonette had been captured and stolen all those years ago. How he'd tracked her down and intended to save her. But had to wait until she grew old enough to run away with him. Her little *Lakey* hadn't been a lizard at all, but a young dragon.

While he recounted the sorry tale, he stroked her arm. When he silenced at last, his hand halted at hers and their fingers entwined. He nuzzled into her neck and whispered, 'I took an oath never to love another. When I knocked you out of the sky, I had no idea it was you. I felt so bad for kissing you—against my vow. But now, my love …'

His lips crashed down onto hers, and she opened into his passion. His tongue lapped at her, while he eased her round until they lay chest to chest. Heat blazed in her abdomen, and trickled down between her legs. He tore at her clothing, until they lay naked on the sheet.

Even with their limbs entwined and entangled like this, it didn't feel close enough for her. She needed more. Inexplicably, he paused. Gave her a considering look. 'You're a virgin.'

Statement, not question.

Bemused, she smiled and asked, 'How do you know that?'

'You've never undergone a transformation. Once you've experienced the fire of your first consummation, you'll shift, like I do.'

'Oh.'

He smiled and nuzzled her nose. 'Ready?'

Jenna nuzzled back. 'Make me fly.'

Their laughter faded out, then changed into moans as each pleasured the other. Twice, she climaxed before he finally thrust his hot, hard, thick length into her. She gripped his shoulders and rocked with him.

Eyes locked on his, she cried out his name as they rode the thermals together.

At last, she'd come home.

CHAPTER FOUR

Tryst

Senior Nurse, Polly Johnson, ogled the Consultant, Cameron Hemingway, while he sauntered down the short corridor that separated the Child Psychiatric Unit from the medical offices and consulting rooms. No matter how many times she saw it, his tight, firm butt thrilled her. Some days, it was all she could manage not to grab it and give it a squeeze. Once, he'd caught her looking.

A loveable doctor, despite being an academic, he had a sharp sense of humour and would never dream of talking-down to anyone, regardless of their station. From the first day she'd set eyes on him, he'd attracted her, with his strong, square jaw, dark eyes, full lips, and toned physique.

With a shake of her head, Polly turned away and headed for the seniors' lounge. The ward took children between five and fifteen, and split them into three groups: Infants—five to eights, Juniors—nines to twelves, and Seniors, thirteens to fifteens. Until last month, she'd worked with the Juniors. Sister liked to rotate the staff between groups every six months to a year, and Polly had just transferred into the Seniors, which took some getting used to—their needs completely opposite to those of the younger kids. Early signs suggested that she might grow to love it.

Her mind drifted back to breakfast that morning. Her partner had brought her coffee in bed and given her a thorough waking up. Oh, for more mornings like that. Polly stifled a giggle. A passing HCA gave her a look, and Polly wondered how much had shown on her face. The two women exchanged nods and smiles and went on their ways.

Over breakfast, she'd reminded her boyfriend of the leaving do tonight, and that she'd be going straight from work. He'd given her a lingering kiss goodbye, which involved feeling her up, and then sent her packing. No wonder she'd arrived at the unit horny.

The day flew by, and it seemed like no time at all before the last child left in a taxi with her escort. Millie, the student nurse, locked the doors and brought the keys back to Polly, who took them with a smile. 'Thanks. You coming tonight?'

The girl grinned and nodded. 'Wouldn't miss it for the world.'

'Me either. I'll miss her, you know. She's been here forever.'

'Yeah, she's like part of the furniture. Do you think she'll cope with retirement?' A frown settled on her face.

Polly shook her head. 'No.' Dot had cried at her final staff appraisal. The woman had turned sixty and had to take mandatory retirement, which didn't sit well with her at all. Hopefully, she'd hold it together tonight. Polly gave a tight smile to the student. 'We've gotten her registered with the nursing pool, so maybe she can come back as Bank Staff when we're short.'

'She can do that? Even though she's retired?'

Polly nodded. 'Yeah, crazy as it seems. She's just not allowed to have a full-time contract with us anymore. Working on the Bank is fine.' A glance at the clock reminded her that they'd best get cracking if they wanted to get there on time.

Ninety minutes saw them dolled up and climbing out of the

cab, ready to hit the town. The unit staff were meeting up in *The Dog and Duck*, and then heading to the *Taste of India* for a meal. Heaven only knew where they'd end up. Polly shoved her way through the crowded lounge and up to the group holding up the bar. Someone shoved a G & T into her hand, which she raised in the air with a grin. 'Cheers,' she said to no one in particular, and a chorus of the same came back.

A half-hour later, and two more G & Ts, everyone who'd said they'd come had come. They made their rowdy way to the exit doors. Just as Polly stepped onto the pavement, she spied Cameron Hemingway. He hadn't mentioned he'd be here—kept that one quiet. He'd changed from his suit to tight-fitting jeans and t-shirt. Polly's pulse sped up, fuelled—no doubt—by the rapid alcohol consumption. Food … she needed food, and soon. Soak up some of the gin.

Over the heads of their little crowd, he caught her eye and gave her a wave and a grin. Then got busy saying his hellos to everyone else. Polly wanted him. No—craved him. It wouldn't do, though. The unit frowned upon relations between staff, and even more so between the doctors and nurses. In Polly's book, it all seemed a tad archaic. Damn her man for sending her to work so wound up.

At the restaurant, staff seated them in a long row, at tables they'd pulled together to allow for the group to sit en-masse. Cameron ended up opposite Polly, and spent a lot of time checking out her cleavage. Even sobered up a little, with the help of the food, Polly felt like she couldn't get through the rest of the night without having him. And his obvious interest stirred her desire further.

After the meal, the group jostled itself back onto the street and headed for *Oceania*, Plymouth's largest nightclub, where someone had, it seemed, reserved a private booth for their party. Cameron wangled his way to her side and bumped her arm. She gave him a glance and a smile, and cursed her fair skin for its tendency to flush. Cameron's dark-chocolate complexion did a good job of hiding any flushing he might have going on.

It had been a while since Polly had felt excitement like this. Her relationship, as long-term alliances were wont to do, had slipped down an embankment and onto a one-way track. Every day, they followed the same schedule, the same route, and their old love-train only detoured if a big enough obstruction forced it to. Tonight, Cameron made her feel young again. Perhaps, this evening, they'd find passion on fun, new tracks.

While they walked, Polly and Cameron slowed their pace so that the rest of the group overtook them. They did this without so much as a word to one another. When the last reveller rounded the corner ahead, he slipped his hand into hers. Only for a second. She squeezed his fingers. Then they reached the corner, and he let her hand go. It felt cold and empty without him.

At the club entrance, Polly and Cameron brought up the rear of the queue and stood to wait while Hilary, the medical secretary, went up to one of the bouncers to show him their VIP pass, which would—apparently—give them instant entry. Cameron shifted close to Polly, and his groin nudged her buttocks. She couldn't help it, she leaned backward, into hard warmth. Then the bouncer—curse him—waved them all forward.

While they checked in their coats and bags, Polly got separated from Cameron. By the time she made it to the upstairs booth, he sat toward the back, hemmed in by David and Laura—two of the junior doctors from the unit. Polly had no option but to slide into a seat on the edge of the group and well away from Cameron. Drat it. Probably for the best, though.

A waitress brought a complementary bottle of Vodka to the table and took drinks orders. Not wanting to mix her grains, Polly stuck with G & T. Suzy, a staff nurse, plonked down into the seat next to Polly, gave her an inebriated nudge, and pointed toward some eye-candy on the dance floor. Tonight, however, Polly only had one man on her mind.

She made a show of joining in the jokes and banter, but

caught his eye every chance she got. Their looks grew hotter until they smouldered across the small space separating them. Polly tried crossing her legs and clenching her thighs, but it got to the point that she couldn't sit there any longer without doing something. She made her excuses and slid out of her seat, intending to go to the ladies' room.

As always, Polly felt vulnerable as soon as she left the crowded main area and entered the darkened and sparsely populated hallway. Her unease increased when a sign directed her through double doors and down ill-lit stairs. Why did they have to put the toilets so out of the way? Behind her, the double doors whooshed open.

Hurried footsteps followed her down the steps, and then a hand took her elbow. She'd know his manly scent anywhere. Cameron. They shared a look. Then he took her hand and steered her past the restrooms and further along the empty corridor. Polly glanced up at him, 'Where are we going?'

He chuckled. 'I'm not sure. I haven't been back here before.' He winked, and then said, 'I don't make a habit of this, you know.'

'I should hope not,' she said, but in a playful tone.

They rounded a corner. About fifteen feet ahead of them, the corridor dead-ended. A door with a 'No Admittance' sign faced them. Just to their left, stood a closed door without any signage. Cameron looked at her and said, 'What do you think? Shall we give it a try?'

Polly grinned. 'I'm game if you are.'

With a glance left and right to ensure they remained unobserved, Cameron twisted the knob and pushed. The door swung open and revealed pitch-darkness. Face set in a nervous frown, he patted the inner wall, looking for a switch. When he found one, the room blazed into light. Polly peered in. A cleaner's cupboard. Before she could change her mind, Cameron pulled her in after him and shut the door. Then he turned the light off again.

By now, Polly had grown soaking wet, and he hadn't even done anything to her yet. Her night blindness enhanced every sound, smell, and touch. His cologne teased her nostrils when he bent and pressed his luscious lips to hers. With a moan of pleasure and anticipation, Polly reached up and grasped the back of his head, fingers splayed through his hair.

His tongue pushed at her lips, and she opened for him. He probed and explored and lapped. With one hand, he held her head in place, and with the other, he reached to her cleavage and fondled one breast, then the next. His lips drifted down her neck, and Polly arched for him, needing more.

Deft hands pulled her dress down until the neckline lay beneath her exposed breasts. He dipped his head and sucked a hard nipple into his hot mouth. Polly moaned. Cameron shared his attention between nipples and moved his hands to her buttocks, which he squeezed through the flimsy fabric of her short black dress. Her hips rocked into him. 'Oh yes.'

'Mmm,' he murmured against her bared skin, and she trembled beneath his lips.

When he pulled away, Polly's nipples pebbled even more as the cool air brushed them, and she whimpered at his desertion. With a low chuckle that had her even wetter, he reached beneath her dress and tugged at her panties. In one smooth move, he had them down to her ankles, where he slipped them over her feet and into one of his pockets.

On his knees in front of her, he pushed up her dress until it bunched around her waist, and then nudged her legs further apart. Polly gasped and bucked when he spread her with his fingers and circled her clit with his tongue. Sweat slicked her back, and cream pumped from her core as he brought her to the edge with his fingers and tongue.

Her knees trembled, and he took her weight on his shoulders while he held her against the wall. He pulled his head back a little. 'Come for me.'

Then he dove in between her thighs again and gave her a thorough fucking with his fingers and tongue. Heat gathered low down, and Polly's core clenched; she was so close. Then he wrapped his lips around her clit and sucked, and Polly had to shove a fist into her mouth to stifle her cries. She came hard while he continued to work his fingers in and out of her. He kept working her until her shudders subsided, and then he eased her down to the floor where he manoeuvred into a sitting position and pulled her into his lap.

He brought his lips to her mouth, and her taste on his tongue triggered fresh arousal. In the darkness, she twisted around until she straddled him. While they explored one another with their tongues, she pulled his t-shirt over his head and ran her hands up and down his naked chest. His six-pack rippled beneath her fingers. When she hooked a digit under his waistband, he moaned and bucked.

'You want me, big boy?' Polly asked, and then moved back to give herself room to kiss her way down his torso. Through his jeans, his erection throbbed against her hand as she stroked his hard length.

'Oh baby,' he said, and moaned when she pulled down his zipper and undid the button. Through the opening, she gave him a squeeze, and then tugged at his jeans. He lifted his hips, and together they wrestled his clothing down to his knees.

Polly wrapped a small hand around his freed shaft—hot and hard—and worked it up and down at a lazy pace. At the tip, she ran a thumb over his slit and smeared his pre-cum down his length as she stroked down to his base once more. Then she took him into her mouth and sucked. He gasped and bucked his hips, and then put his hands on the back of her head. 'Oh baby.'

Nearly at her second climax, just from pleasuring him, Polly worked her hand and mouth up and down his length. His cock pulsed and twitched, and he eased her mouth off him. 'I'm close,' he said.

'I want you to come.'

He sucked in a breath. 'Are you sure?'

'I want to taste you. Come in my mouth.'

A groan vibrated into the darkness, and Cameron cupped each side of her head while she lowered her mouth to his groin and sucked his thick length into her. Within seconds, the pressure built too high for him to stay still while she ministered to him, and he gripped her ears and thrust until his balls slapped at her chin and his tip massaged the back of her throat. Polly groaned around him, and he twitched again. His thrusts grew faster. Then his cock pulsed, and he squirted his release into her. 'Oh fuck,' he cried, rather loudly, considering the circumstances.

For a moment, they both froze and listened, but when half a minute passed without anyone discovering them, they relaxed. Polly erupted into giggles and had to let his softening member slip from her lips. Cameron pulled her back onto his lap, where she curled up, and they exchanged soft chuckles and kisses.

He gave them a few minutes like this, and then said, 'We should get back before they miss us.'

With a sigh, Polly agreed, and they got busy putting themselves to rights again. He risked the light so they could see what they were doing, but snuffed it before he eased open the door to peek down the corridor. All clear. Polly snuck out first and made her way to the ladies.

By the time she got back to the booth, half the party had moved to the dance floor, and nobody batted an eyelid when she slipped back into her seat and retrieved her half-emptied G & T. A few minutes later, Cameron arrived with a waitress in tow and organised another round of drinks for everyone. The man knew how to cover up.

They avoided looking at one another for the most part, which Polly found difficult. Despite her orgasm in the cupboard, her core ached for more. She half regretted letting him finish in her mouth, as she could have done with him filling her instead. All she could think about was having him inside her, stretching her as wide as she would go. He was a big man.

Her libido hadn't been this active in quite some time. Even though she'd had sex twice today, she felt like it'd been forever without any. At some point, unable to sit still, Polly joined the crowd on the dance floor and lost herself to the music.

A little after one in the morning, Hilary tapped her on the shoulder and mouthed, 'We're going.' Polly nodded. Their group had a standing agreement that everyone stayed together, and that no one would ever be left behind.

Outside, Polly shivered in the cold while everyone got

themselves organised and decided who would share a taxi with whom. Six of their group remained when Cameron came and stood by her side. Not caring about curious eyes or loose lips, he bent and kissed her. A full, passionate kiss, with his tongue wrapped around hers.

Millie, the student, gasped, but Polly ignored the girl. Right now, she'd gotten past caring what any of them thought or said. Mike, one of the E-grades, whistled between his teeth, and Janet laughed and said, 'Get a room.'

Polly and Cameron pulled apart and joined in with the banter. Only Millie looked scandalised, but then—of course—she didn't know. Only the old-timers knew. Polly kept her private life well away from work … usually. Tonight was the first time in nearly five years that they'd let their guard down in front of their colleagues.

Another taxi pulled into the rank, and the remaining four members of staff headed over to it. Millie got in first and said something that Polly didn't catch. Janet looked over her shoulder at Polly, grinned, waved, turned to face the student, and then said loud enough for her voice to carry, 'They're partners, you doofus. They just don't bring it to work.'

Polly glanced through the side window of the car. Millie's mouth formed a perfect 'O'. Cameron laughed, and wrapped his arms around Polly's shoulders from behind. She leaned into him, and he nuzzled her neck. 'Your place or mine?' he whispered into her ear.

'Ooh, let me think.' She giggled. 'Will your girlfriend be home?'

'Nah. She's out at some work leaving do. And you know what those nurses are like.'

'Yeah. Just as bad as those doctor types.'

He lowered his hands to her waist and tickled her. Polly screeched and squirmed in his strong arms, then twisted around until she stood facing him. He kissed the cold away until a free cab pulled into the taxi rank.

Back home, Polly brewed coffee while Cameron checked the answer-phone. With nothing urgent waiting, they prepared to go bed. Tonight had been so wonderful, and Polly worried a little that they would just slip back into their usual routine now they were home.

A mug of coffee in each hand, Polly made her way through the bungalow, switching off lights with a nudge of her elbow as she went. Cameron had gone ahead of her to perform his nightly ablutions, and had taken a bottle of water for each of them to bed. With the amount of alcohol they'd imbibed, they were sure to need hydrating through the night.

With her knee, Polly shoved the bedroom door open, and then paused, staring. Cameron lay on top of the duvet, naked, and aroused. His cock twitched and poked into the air.

She grinned and raised the mugs, 'I guess you won't be wanting coffee, then?'

He lay with his hands clasped behind his head. 'I thought you might need a bit of protein—keep your strength up for all that hot sex you're gonna give me.'

Polly crossed to her side of the bed and set the mugs down on the nightstand. With a wicked gleam in her eye, she told him, 'Nah. I got off with this stud of a doctor earlier tonight. Not sure if I can handle any more meat just yet.'

A loud guffaw rumbled out of his chest and went straight to the hot, wet place between her thighs. Then he sprang to his knees, grabbed her, and pulled her—giggling—onto the mattress, where he pinned her beneath him. His knee nudged between hers and pushed her legs apart. The rest of him followed.

Careful to hold most of his weight above her, he covered her and dipped his head for a kiss. It started slow—long and lingering—and then the passion hijacked them. In no time at all, and hardly breaking off the kiss, he divested her of her dress, then her bra, and—finally—her panties. Without the thin fabric to soak up her wetness, moisture soon coated her upper thighs.

Cameron kissed one leg, then the other, and breathed in deep. 'Mmm, I love your smell.' Then he slid back up her body and slipped his tongue into her mouth.

When he came back up for air, Polly said, 'Just my smell,

huh?'

All at once, the fun fled and a serious expression settled onto his face. Concerned, Polly asked, 'What is it?'

He stroked her chin, and then pecked her on the lips. The silence stretched for about ten seconds while he looked down at her. Then he lifted away from her and eased to his feet by the bed. Perturbed, Polly sat up and swung her legs over the edge of the mattress. 'Cameron?'

Without a word, he bent down and pulled open the drawer in his nightstand. After he'd closed it again, he turned to face her. Naked, and his erection bouncing in the air, he knelt and took her hand.

Then she got it. Tears sprang to her eyes. Cameron gazed up at her. 'My darling. I love you. All of you. I would be the happiest man on Earth if you consented to be my wife.'

'Oh, Cameron!' She threw her arms around him and pulled him up and into a kiss.

'Well?' he asked, back on his knees in front of her.

'Yes.' She sniffled. 'Yes, you great oaf, of course I will.'

His eyes sparkled as he opened the small velvet-covered box he held in his palm. A diamond engagement ring glinted in the lamplight. Cameron lifted it from its white satin cushion and slipped it onto her ring finger. A perfect fit. Polly raised her eyebrows.

Cameron kissed her, and then smiled. 'I managed to measure it one night while you slept. Twice, you nearly woke up. Scared the living shit out of me. I so wanted it to be a surprise.'

Polly wiped at a stray tear that had escaped to her cheek, and then pulled him onto the bed next to her. His lips crashed down onto hers, and they fell backward to the mattress together, limbs entangled.

Mischief as well as passion sang through her veins. She grinned. He paused in his caresses with a look of suspicion narrowing his eyes, but—still—he couldn't contain his own grin. 'What?'

'Oh, I was just thinking about what a story your proposal will make.' Polly giggled.

He tried to keep a straight face while he attempted to rewrite recent history, 'Getting down on one knee is so old hat. Nobody will care.'

'Not until I mention the bit about you being in your birthday suit while you did it.'

'You wouldn't dare.'

'Mmm, a bit of bribery for my silence might do the trick.'

'Bitch,' he said with a laugh.

On her back, she lay there and locked eyes with his. 'Fuck me.'

His cock twitched, and he groaned. 'I'm gonna make you beg.' Then he bent down to tease her with his tongue.

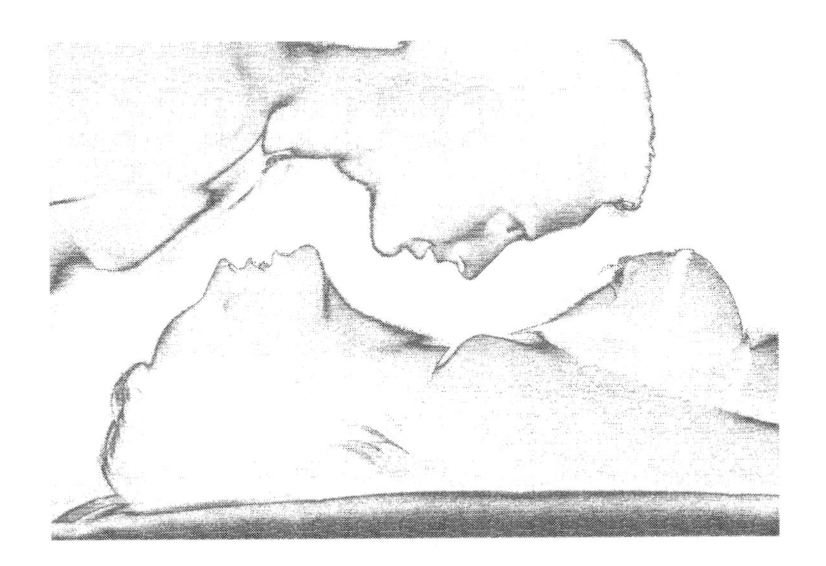

CHAPTER FIVE

Love on the Cornish Line

Becky, carried by the flow of the harried, home-bound throng around her, caught her low work heel on the uneven tarmac and went down. A full, mortifying face plant in the grit. Talk about being alone in a crowd—not one person stopped to help. Feet sidestepped around her, and a couple of people paused to stare before swiftly moving on. Meanwhile, stunned and with the wind knocked from her, Becky lay there, sprawled flat on her stomach, with her arms and legs flung out to the four points of the compass and gravel embedded in her right cheek.

While she tried to regain her wits and forcibly suppress a self-pitying sob of frustration and embarrassment, a hand rested on her shoulder, and a gentle voice asked, 'Are you okay, miss?'

Becky raised her face from the dirt and blinked. The low winter sun hung behind her would-be helper and left him in silhouette. 'I think so,' she said, wriggling to all fours. However, when she tried to push herself to her feet, her ankle gave way and screamed at her. White heat shot up through her calf and she collapsed onto her backside.

The man who'd knelt beside her shifted and gripped her elbow, looking down at her intently. 'Does it feel broken?'

Apprehensive, Becky twirled it, and while it hurt like the dickens, it didn't grate and she had control of it. 'I don't think so.'

His altered position allowed her to see more of his features. Hopeless at guessing ages as she was, she assumed him to be roughly a decade older than her, and handsome. His chiselled chin held a shadow of stubble, which hugged full lips, and his pale blue eyes looked kind. He bent his face close to hers. 'May I help you up?'

Becky nodded, even while cringing in anticipation of the expected pain. The man raised to his feet and nudged a foot against her uninjured one, ready to brace her. Then he took hold of her hands and waited for her to nod her readiness. In one heave—God, but he must have muscles—he pulled her to her feet and grabbed her when she stumbled into him. His chest felt firm and warm, and his heart beat steadily against her.

Even while her ankle throbbed and smarted, Becky wondered if he was married. Most likely. That was the story of her life. At forty, all the good guys were taken already. And no matter how well she got on with her friends, being single amidst all those couples did get in the way. Take this weekend, for example. Three of her married friends and their spouses had gone away as a group to a hotel for a romantic Valentine's weekend of pampering. Because Becky didn't have a fella, they hadn't invited her along on the assumption that she'd feel out of place. True, she probably would, but was feeling left out any better? With a shrug, Becky tried again to pull herself together. Her friends had it right—she would have been in the way; a spare wheel that would've changed the atmosphere for all of them. She smiled and wished, again, that they all had a great time. Fed up as she felt with her life, she did want her mates to be happy.

Still gripping her just above her elbows and holding her against his torso, tall-muscled-saviour leaned back to look down at her, concern warming his eyes. 'How's that feel?'

Fucking brilliant. At the last second, she managed to hold that in, and instead settled for, 'Um, I'm not sure I can walk on it.'

'If I help, do you think you can put a bit of weight on it?'

Not seeing any other options, and grateful for his offer, Becky nodded. 'Yes, please.'

He eased her arm around his neck and shoved his shoulder beneath her underarm, which—due to his foot of height above her—felt awkward, to say the least. 'I'm Eddie, by the way.'

'Um, Becky. Hi.'

A soft, deep bass chuckle rumbled out of him and did things to her insides. 'Which train were you headed for?'

It took Becky a few moments to get her brain on track. 'The five-fifty to Plymouth.' Becky paused, unsure how much information Eddie wanted, then shrugged and said, 'I'm heading for Lostwithiel, eventually—I change at Plymouth.'

Eddie smiled and raised his eyebrows. 'A romantic weekend getaway?'

Without thinking, Becky blurted, 'I wish.' Then blushed furiously. After a gulp, in which she wished the floor would just open up and swallow her whole, she said, 'I live not too far out of Lostwithiel. This is my weekly commute. I can't tell you how much I wait for the weekends where I can get out of the hustle and bustle …' Mortified anew at her rambling, she clamped her lips shut with a vow of lifelong silence from here on in.

Eddie's eyes widened a little in surprise, and his smile broadened. 'Huh. That's a nice coincidence. I'm heading there too.' He paused, looked uncomfortable, and then added, 'I better tell you now so you don't think I'm stalking you or anything.'

Despite herself, Becky smiled and asked, 'Where do you live?'—Happy for once at the gender inequality that made it okay for her to ask him, while for him to ask her might be considered creepy.

'Lerryn. Do you know it?'

Becky gasped and nodded. 'Yeah. I live just up the valley. At the highway.'

Recognition lit his features. 'How come I've never seen you around?'

Becky licked her lips. 'Well, I only moved there about a year ago, and I'm only there weekends. Still finding my feet … hah, if you'll pardon the pun.'

Eddie chuckled, and then frowned after he checked his watch. 'We'd best get going if we want to catch our train.'

'Um, yeah, thanks.'

As expected, her ankle hurt real bad with every hobbling step. Eddie took as much of her weight as he could, though, and together they made slow progress toward platform three. At the end of the waiting train, Eddie asked, 'Which carriage?'

A little embarrassed at the extravagance, Becky mumbled, 'Um, first class, please.'

Eddie smiled. 'I like a lady who travels in style.'

While they shuffle-hobbled down the length of the train, searching for the access doors to the first-class carriage, Eddie chuckled.

'What?' Becky felt so self-conscious.

'Oh, just all the coincidences tonight. If I were superstitious …'

Becky sucked a breath in. 'You're not telling me that not only do you live a mile away from me, but you're travelling first class too?'

He paused mid-step and Becky looked up at him to see him blushing slightly. 'Yes, as a matter of fact. I swear, I didn't set this up.'

Now it was her turn to chuckle. 'I believe you. I tell you, if this was fiction, people would say it's too unbelievable—too convenient.'

'Convenient?'

Now she flushed deep crimson. Shit. Talk about foot in mouth. 'Um, nothing.' Then, almost under her breath, she said,

'You're probably married anyway.'

Eddie gave a startled laugh, loud and hearty. 'Nope, I'm single. Divorced three years. You?'

So ready to die, Becky stammered, 'Er, um, I—no, I'm not married. Not divorced either. Never found the right guy, I suppose. Er … oh hell, I never meant to say that out loud—about you probably being married … I … oh hell.'

Eddie eased himself into a position directly facing her and held onto her elbows again. 'You don't need to be embarrassed around me. Not ever.'

The look in his eyes had her heart melting and her knees going weak, and she held onto his arms for dear life. And, damn her eyes, she had to blink back tears. What was wrong with her? Rebecca Caytor, CEO of Comtech UK, did not cry … not ever. Strong, resilient, a bitch when necessary, she had her life mapped out—all except for the romantic part; it seemed that her success didn't include her love life. To cover, her humour came to the fore, and she came out with a totally random thought. 'I should've known you were Cornish right away.'

His gaze shifted to curiosity. 'Why would you have known that? I didn't think my accent was that strong.'

She shook her head. 'It's not. I mean, if I listen for it, I can hear it. But that's not what gave you away.'

His smile crept up, soft and timid. 'What then?'

'Your kindness.' She flushed some more. This had turned too serious, too quickly. 'Out of all those people, you're the only one who stopped to help.' Becky shook her head. 'That's the first thing I noticed after I moved to the Southwest. How kind and generous folks are. Being an incomer, it's slow going to fit in, but I've made some good friends who've accepted me just as I am. And they're loyal. Even after such a short time, I don't think I could live anywhere else. The sense of community—well, at least in rural Cornwall—is like stepping back twenty or thirty years, especially compared with somewhere like London. I've never felt so isolated as when I'm here.'

Eddie nodded, and a sad look shadowed his eyes. 'I'm Cornish born and bred, and I've hated every minute I've spent away.'

Curious, Becky asked, 'Why're you here, then?'

Eddie's expression softened, and he said, 'Tell you what, why don't we talk about it during the journey. I'm sure we can get seats together for the ride. I'll tell you mine if you tell me yours.'

With a quiet laugh, Becky nodded. 'You're on, mister.'

Once again, he hooked his shoulder under her arm and they shuffled off again.

By the time they reached the first class carriage, it felt utterly beyond her to climb up the step to access the train. With a whispered, 'Let me,' Eddie scooped her into his arms and lifted her through the open doors. In that moment, Becky fell in love with the tall, handsome, kind stranger. Until then, she'd scoffed at the notion of love at first sight, but there you go. The fact that he wasn't married still struggled to sink through the hard veneer of her hard-won cynicism, and a little voice whispered that there must be something wrong with him. If she could have kicked herself right then, she would have done, with vigour.

Once they got into the carriage, Becky managed to help herself along by holding onto the seat backs as she made her way down the aisle. Eddie stayed on her heels, and they secured seats side-by-side in the near-empty compartment. With only two minutes until departure, it seemed unlikely that anyone would turn up with a pre-booked seat demanding that they move. And, even if they did, plenty of other vacant seating offered itself.

Oh, the utter relief when Becky eased herself down into the plush chair and got the weight off her leg. Eddie dropped down next to her, after putting their bags beneath the table in front of them, and then he leant forward and slipped off her shoe. When she didn't protest, he lifted her foot into his lap and, with tender fingers, massaged her ankle. Becky felt self-conscious at how sweaty her thigh-high hosiery must smell by the end of her work day, and she pulled her foot back a little. 'My feet are all smelly and gross,' she said.

To her horror, he lifted her foot to his face and sniffed. Then, after mock gasping for air, he smiled and reassured her, 'I can live with it if you can. Believe me, I've experienced a lot worse.'

Becky snorted. Yep, actually snorted. Oh boy. 'I'm not sure how to take that.'

Eddie recommenced rubbing her swollen ankle and said, 'I grew up on a farm.'

'Ah, 'nough said.'

They sat in companionable silence for a couple of minutes while a few more passengers boarded, and the train got underway. Once it got up to speed, the rhythmic rocking and ca-thunk of its motion felt soothing to Becky, and she rested her head back on the headrest with a sigh. Eyes closed, she asked, 'What brings you to London, then? If you grew up on a farm.'

Eddie worked his hand at her ankle and lower calf. 'The youngest son, and all that. Pete took over the running. Not really enough to sustain all of us, and when he got married and started a family …'

'Time for you to leave the nest.'

'You got it.'

Becky cracked one eye open and watched Eddie. 'What do you do now?'

He glanced at her with a relaxed smile. 'IT consultant. You?'

Becky took a deep breath in. Usually, she kept her job description vague, not wanting to let people know she was a high earner, but with Eddie she wanted to be honest and up front. 'CEO at Comtech UK.'

His expression didn't change, and nor did the rhythm of his hand on her leg. All good. She relaxed more and closed her eyes again. The fact he'd taken that in his stride meant a lot to her. Then a thought drifted through. 'I expect that you're quite high up the food chain yourself by now?'

For answer, Eddie chuckled and squeezed her calf muscle. Then he asked, 'Is it important?' His false nonchalance didn't fool her for even a second.

'Just curious.' His massage felt so good. A sigh escaped, and Becky slouched in her seat.

'Curiosity killed the cat.' With those words, Eddie gave her leg a squeeze just below her knee, and when Becky opened her eyes, he met her gaze with a wicked grin, which Becky returned.

'You gonna tell me you're an axe murderer in your spare time?'

Eddie laughed and waggled his eyebrows. 'Nothing wrong with a good old bit of blood lust.'

His hand came to rest on her knee, just at the hemline of her pencil skirt, and his eyes locked with hers. A look passed between them, and electricity filled the air. Becky's heart sped up and heat pooled low in her belly. All at once, their mood turned a lot more serious. Then Eddie blinked and edged his hand back toward her ankle. Becky leaned over and laid her palm on his arm. 'It's okay,' she said at a near whisper. Then, after a loud swallow, she said, 'I'm enjoying it.'

Still watching her intently, he slid his hand up her shin until it rested on her knee again. In a soft voice, he asked, 'How's that feeling?'

With a sigh, Becky murmured, 'Pretty damn good.'

Eddie sucked in air, and his hand twitched on her leg. 'And what about the ankle?'

Becky laughed and closed her eyes, needing to break the intense moment even just a little. 'Oh, I've forgotten all about that.'

Eddie laughed with her, and they both relaxed. The remainder of the journey to Plymouth passed with them swapping life anecdotes and getting to know one another. Eddie massaged her leg the whole time, but didn't go any higher than her knee, and kept it clean and above board. Even while she respected him for not coming on to her, she also felt a little disappointed. Once they changed trains, their journey would be over all too soon.

When they disembarked, Eddie climbed from the carriage first and helped Becky down to the platform. Her ankle still twinged, but nothing like it had done. With her arm linked through his, and Eddie carrying their bags, they made their way through the station to hunt down the train that would take them to the tiny station at Lostwithiel.

When they boarded the end carriage, only two other people

shared the space, and one of those got off at the Bodmin Parkway. Their route home took them via the Brownqueen tunnel, over the river Fowey, and Becky hated that she would have to leave Eddie's company all too soon. Then providence struck.

At just eighty metres, the tunnel wasn't so long, and they should have been through it in no time, but the train slowed until it came to a stop mid-tunnel. Then the lights went out. Alarmed, Becky sat up straight and gripped Eddie's knee without thinking about it. His warm hand came down over hers and held it. Then his breath tickled her ear when he whispered, 'I'm sure it's okay. Do you want me to find the guard?'

Uselessly in the darkness, Becky shook her head. 'No. Um, stay with me?'

The silence held his surprise. Becky said, 'Don't laugh, but I don't like the dark. I mean, I'm fine at home, but …'

Eddie finished for her, 'Unknown place, unknown people.' He squeezed her knee. 'If it helps, I'm not going anywhere.'

Becky let her breath out in a whoosh. 'That helps.'

At her knee, his hand squeezed again, and then his soft lips brushed her cheek. Next, she felt his arm easing behind her neck. 'Snuggle in. I got you.' Becky relaxed and did as he suggested, sinking gratefully into him. Strangers though they were, she trusted him implicitly and welcomed being close to him. Maybe with this darkness, she might get a bit bolder?

Becky twisted her head to snuggle into his neck, and murmured, 'Thank you.' Then she planted a brief kiss to his flesh.

Next to her, Eddie tensed, then he let out a long, slow exhale and kissed the top of her head. When he pulled away, she wondered if she'd gone too far too soon. Then, after a bit of rustling at floor level, he pulled her back into a cuddle, while his other hand activated the torch on his mobile phone. In its light, he studied her, and the sexual tension between them mounted. Becky licked her lips and asked, 'What is it? I'm sorry if—'

A finger to her lips silenced her. Then he brought his nose to hers and whispered, 'I want to kiss you so badly right now.'

With a soft moan of want, Becky parted her lips, and her

eyes slid to half-lidded. Eddie leant in and brushed his mouth over hers. When he pulled away, Becky took the initiative and reciprocated. Then he hooked his hand in her hair at the nape of her neck and deepened the embrace. His tongue nudged at her lips, and she opened for him. The kiss came slow, lingering, and sensuous, and by the time they came up for air, they were both panting. Just then, the guard entered the carriage and spoke to the three occupants.

'Sorry for the delay, folks, and the power outage. We're experiencing mechanical problems. We'll be underway as soon as possible.'

The man behind them asked, 'How long are we going to be?'

The guard held a polite smile and repeated that they'd get moving ASAP, then he turned and left. Just as the door slid shut behind him, Eddie's phone gave a double beep. 'Ah hell. Battery's low.' With a pained look, he switched it off and plunged them into pitch-blackness once more. 'Do you have a light on yours?'

Becky, half-welcoming the return to blindness after their kiss, felt happy at having to admit, 'Mine needs recharging as well. I didn't get chance at work today.'

When Eddie spoke, Becky could hear the smile in his voice, 'Well then, I guess we'll just have to stay close.'

With a soft chuckle, Becky said, 'If we must.' Then she fumbled around in the darkness until she found his lips again. Then the passenger behind them lit the torch on his phone. Damn technology. With a sigh, they parted. Then Eddie sunk lower into the seat, so the headrests screened them somewhat, and Becky followed suit. But with the extra illumination, they both felt more self-conscious, especially with the occasional complaints and grumbles that burst from the other man.

An uncomfortable half-hour passed, then the man got up, with more curses, and stomped out of the carriage, all the while muttering about going to find out who was in charge. The light went with him, and Eddie wasted no time in finding Becky's mouth again. This time, when his hand went to her knee, he didn't seem to have the same inhibitions about keeping it there, and while their tongues wrapped around one another, he slid up to mid thigh and squeezed.

Heat and liquid flooded her girl parts, and Becky no longer lamented being so close to home. She wanted him. Dare she go there, though? Now, her regret turned to the delay that would mean she couldn't answer her question for the foreseeable future. Not unless she got ultra-daring. Could she? Her body answered for her, and she parted her legs as much as her slim skirt would allow, to give his hand room to roam. Eddie moaned into her mouth, and the kiss moved into full on passion. The kind of passion that led to bed and sweaty bodies and tangled limbs.

Eddie's free hand found the mounds of her breasts through her thin blouse and cupped her, then his thumb ran over her nipples, which hardened at his touch. Becky arched her back and thrust her chest into him while she moaned with the pleasure that shot from her nipples to her core. Becky dropped her hand to his lap and rubbed the erection that tented his suit trousers.

With a gasp, Eddie broke the kiss and disentangled his hands. 'We'd better stop.' Everything in his tone of voice told her that desisting was the last thing he wanted to do. Then his lips crashed down onto hers again, and his tongue plundered her mouth. Then, with a soft curse, he pulled away. 'I'm sorry.'

Becky reached for the back of his head and pulled him in. 'Don't be,' she whispered against his mouth.

After a chaste kiss, he breathed against her lips, 'I'm getting a bit carried away here.'

'I want you to.' Then she took charge and pushed her tongue at the seam of his lips, and he opened for her while his hands roamed some more. With newfound boldness, Becky found the hard bulge in his lap again and rubbed at him through his trousers. Eddie groaned into her mouth, and the hand beneath her skirt pushed higher until he met her panties. Her soaking wet panties.

'Oh fuck,' he murmured into her mouth.

Beyond speech, Becky wriggled her skirt higher to give her room to open a little wider for him, and then he slipped the wet band of fabric to one side. When his fingers nudged at her slick folds, Becky writhed and moaned and bit his bottom lip. Then he pushed a finger into her, and she bucked as hot desire set her on fire. He slid in and out of her and crooked his digit to catch the front of her inner wall and stimulate her g-spot, and his thumb circled her clit. Tongues licking and sucking at each other, his other hand fondled her breasts, and then he reached inside her blouse and bra and twirled a hard nipple between thumb and forefinger.

Oh good God.

An orgasm ripped through her, and she cried out into his mouth. Eddie didn't let up, but rode the wave with her and penetrated her with his finger until she flopped against him, whimpering and panting. Into her neck, he murmured, 'Oh baby.' And then he nuzzled at the soft, tender flesh where shoulder met neck. Beneath her hand, his hard cock twitched. 'So hot and wet for me.' He nuzzled her some more, and Becky squirmed with fresh arousal.

Alone, in a dark carriage. … Could they? Could she? The risk of discovery turned her on even more, and juices slicked from her and soaked her panties. Finger still inside her, Eddie felt the change and slid an extra digit into her. Becky needed more. 'Take me.'

He stilled. 'What if someone comes?'

Becky giggled. 'I fully intend for both of us to come.'

Eddie joined her laughter. 'Are you sure? I mean, God, I want you—so badly—but I've never … have you?'

'I've never so much as kissed anybody on a train, or any public place—held hands and had a quick peck, but this is definitely a first. It's all your fault.'

'Mine?' He sounded incredulous but in an amused way. His lips found hers again while he did things to her with his hands.

Impatient, and thoroughly wanton, Becky pulled down his zipper and unhooked his button. Thin cotton boxers met her hand, and Becky reached into them and pulled him free. He felt hot, hard, and thick. When she gripped him and worked up and down his length, he moaned into her mouth. Becky tried again, 'Take me. I need you inside me.'

'Oh fuck, baby.'

Eager hands took hold of her waist and they manoeuvred until she'd slipped out of her panties and straddled him. His erection rubbed at her slick entrance as she rolled her hips above him. 'Hold on,' he said in a tight voice, and then he fidgeted in the darkness. 'Will you think less of me if I tell you I've got a condom in my wallet?'

'I'd think less of you if you didn't,' she told him, then kissed him.

Eddie shifted in the darkness, and the sound of the foil wrapper ripping reached Becky's ears. Then he pressed at her entrance again. 'Are you sure about this? I want you, but I'll stop.'

'I've never been more sure of anything in my life.' And, risky and daring as this was, she'd never said anything truer. Still, she felt exposed straddling him like this, with her back to the carriage doors. Then she had an idea. She wriggled off his lap and said, 'Come with me.' In the pitch-blackness, she reached for his hand and pulled him across to the facing seats. Her knees bumped the edge, and she climbed into a kneeling position on the thin padding. This local train had nowhere near the luxury of the mainline first-class coach.

Becky gripped the headrest in front of her while Eddie used his hands to feel out her new position. Then he got it, 'We'll see anyone coming through the next carriage now.'

With a twist of her head, she kissed him and then said, 'You got it, cowboy. Now, please, take me, before you find out you're not the only axe murderer in town.'

'Patience, dear heart.' He nuzzled her neck while reaching between her legs and rubbing her clit. Becky moaned and writhed, wet and ready and desperate to have him filling her.

Just when she felt like she would spontaneously combust with the heat of the desire raging through her, he positioned himself at her entrance, then took hold of her hips and thrust into her. The fit was tight and delicious, and she clenched around him. 'Oh yes.'

Eddie nipped her neck and told her, 'Oh baby, you feel so fucking good.'

He pulled back, almost slipping out, then plunged into her.

Each time he penetrated her, he took her harder and increased the tempo of his thrusts. The seat squeaked beneath them, and the carriage rocked a little. Becky muffled her cries by burying her head into the seat rest and biting her tongue. She'd be sore later, but it was so worth it. From behind, Eddie hammered into her over and over, sliding through her slick heat.

Every muscle in her body tightened, and heat built in her abdomen and between her legs. Her nerves tingled and grew super-sensitive. Eddie bit her earlobe and warned her, 'I'm not gonna last much longer.'

Becky reached for one of his hands, lifted it from her hip, and eased it across her belly. He got the message and slipped it between her legs. Then he pinched her clit between his thumb and forefinger and rolled it. Lightning shot up her spine, and she stiffened in his arms while he continued to pummel into her, his breath hot on her neck. When she came, she saw stars, and her core clenched tight around his cock, milking him. In two more thrusts, he joined her and grunted into her neck, 'Oh fuck.' Then he stilled behind her and rested his chin on her shoulder, trying to bring his breathing under control.

A couple of minutes later, through the glass panel in the sliding carriage door, a light appeared and drew closer. 'Shit,' Becky said and giggled. 'We need to move.'

Eddie leapt to his feet and stumbled to the seats behind them. His zipper added to the noises of frantic dressing while Becky yanked her skirt down from her waist and set herself to rights. Then she slid into the seat next to Eddie. 'Oh shit. My knickers.'

'In my pocket,' Eddie whispered, just as the door whooshed open and a silhouette loomed behind torchlight.

The guard spoke, 'Sorry for the long wait. An engine's coming to give us a tow. You folks all right in here?'

They assured him they were fine, and he left them to it. Alone again, Eddie fussed over her. Becky wriggled into her knickers and snuggled into him, feeling content. They agreed that he would follow her home from the station to make sure she got in safely.

'That won't do,' Becky told him.

'No?'

'No. I reckon I'll need a night nurse. I can't be on my own with my ankle like this ...'

His sexy chuckle preceded an even sexier kiss. 'I'm sure something can be arranged,' he said, and came in for another kiss in the dark.

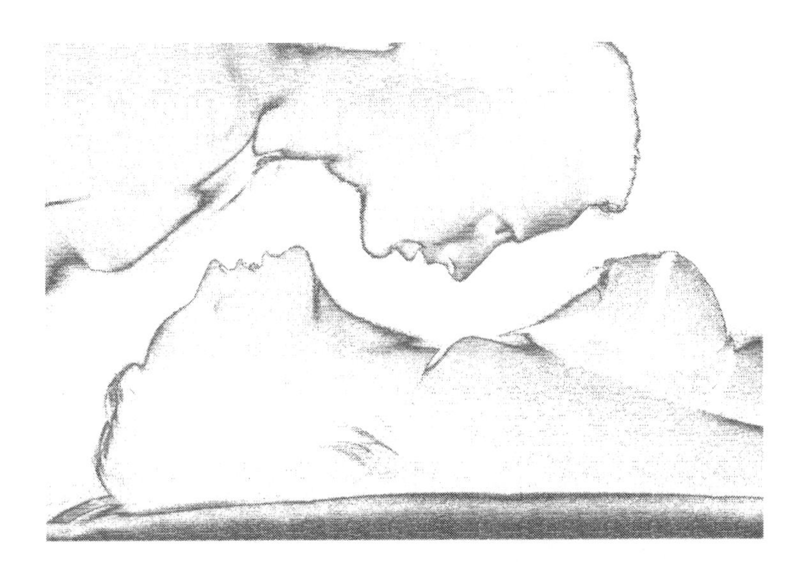

CHAPTER SIX

The Inlaw

When Emma Thornton introduced her boyfriend, Jake Walker, to her mom, Carla had to admit that her daughter had good taste in guys. A self-made man with all the right attributes, she wondered if he had a brother. Turns out, he did. John looked quite the hunk in his best-man's tux, and even more so later at the wedding party when he discarded the jacket and tie and unbuttoned his shirt to reveal a tantalising glimpse of toned, light chocolate skin, which peeked out from behind soft chest hair. Him being twenty years her junior prevented Carla from making any overt approaches, but he served her well as good fantasy fodder over the next weeks.

At forty-three, divorced, and an amputee, she didn't imagine that any guy would be interested again, but—unfortunately—her libido hadn't gotten the memo. A little embarrassed and a lot desperate, she went onto the Ann Summers' website and got a shock at the sheer number of different vibrators and other stuff available. In the end, having checked out the reviews, Carla ordered one of the new Rabbit Vibrators, and prayed that the company's promise of anonymous delivery in unmarked packaging would prove true. She'd die if the postman handed it to her with a knowing grin while the Ann Summers logo did a jolly jig on the box. Happily, when the much dreaded, much anticipated knock on the door came, her postie handed a plain box to her and took her signature without the slightest interest.

Still not quite able to believe she'd bought the thing, Carla unwrapped the package. She gawped. God, the thing was *huge.* What had she done? Not having sex in way too many years meant that things down there had shrunk, and she doubted this beast would even fit. With a shake of her head, she studied the bottle of lube that she'd bought as well. For her age, she remained entirely too innocent in all things sexual. She'd married young, after meeting her fella at work, and so had known only one partner in her life. Listening to friends, Carla realised that her husband wasn't all that adventurous. Most of her carnal knowledge, and fantasies, came from the many erotic books she'd devoured over the years. How sad was she?

The thought of starting anew filled her with fear. Carla seemed to have turned into a pendulum—one minute thinking that she'd quite like to have a boyfriend; someone to snuggle in with of a night, and the next minute swinging to the other side and thinking that, actually, men were more trouble than they were worth and she was better off alone. Better to have a Rabbit she couldn't handle than a man she couldn't handle. Yeah, right. Like she totally believed that.

Intimidated, Carla shoved the vibrator, lube, and freshening wipes into the drawer of her bedside cabinet. When she'd flicked through its different buzz settings and wot-not, it had scared her half to death with how powerful it felt, and that was just in her hand. And, truly, the thing was nothing like a *real* one … it was so hard and unyielding … and, did men *really* come that big? Just what had she been missing out on with Eric?

Carla sighed, resigned that she'd probably just wasted fifty-quid because she'd never use the thing. Her misgivings proved for naught, though. That very night, she lay in bed on her back dreaming about John Walker while her fingers got busy. It just wasn't doing it for her, however, so she got brave and retrieved the beast from the drawer. She'd been right—it was big. Took her ages to stretch around it, and about three nights in a row before she could slide it in to its full length and get the benefit from those delicious rabbit ears. OMG. Whoever came up with *that* idea deserved a knighthood. The bunny became her new best friend.

Life went on nice and smoothly until Emma brought the son-in-law home for a weekend—along with his brother. What did being the brother of her son-in-law make him to Carla? She shook her head, having no clue. Easier just to call him an in-law without getting too specific. All of this mental chatter, of course, was simply a subterfuge to distract her brain from going certain other places with John. The man was so hot, Carla felt in imminent danger of first-degree burns. In fact, every time she so much as glanced in his direction, she got blisters between her legs.

The three youngsters had taken over the back garden to make the most of the summer sun. In a short, strappy summer dress, Carla headed inside to put a tray of cold drinks together. On her way through the patio doors, a deep male voice drifted to her on the breeze. One that she felt convinced she hadn't been meant to overhear. 'Now there's a MILF, if ever there was one.'

Carla recognised Jake's chuckle, which came at the same time as Emma's horrified, '*John!*' Her daughter can't have been that shocked, though, because she followed up with a giggle. Carla flushed. So, hot John thought she was sexy did he? The last thing she'd expected any young guy to say was that she was a mother he'd like to fuck. Wow.

Her abdomen clenched while heat pooled down low. Quite apart from sating her desire, the bunny sessions had taken on a life of their own, and Carla's fantasies had grown more detailed and daring. These days, it seemed like a bloody cucumber was enough to turn her on, never mind hearing a gorgeous twenty-three-year-old guy talking about her like that.

More frustrated and aroused by the second, Carla tried to focus on getting the drinks together. No way could she return to the garden and the … *kids* … feeling like this, though. And not even an ice-cube down her cleavage cooled her off. Jittery and in dire need of a private moment, Carla made a dash for her home-office, which sat at the back of the house.

The cooler air of the small room felt refreshing and welcoming, and Carla felt relieved that she'd closed the blinds against the midday sun before it could turn the office into an oven. Vague ideas of spending the afternoon working had visited, as she felt sure the guys wouldn't want the mother-in-law hanging around them all the time, but right then work was the last thing on her mind.

Cheeks flushed, a sheen of sweat glistening on her skin, Carla sank into her office chair and took a couple of deep breaths. The attempts to calm the raging inferno didn't help any, and nor did her mild-horror at the thought of masturbating in the middle of the day, in her office, with guests sitting just outside. Wanton woman that she'd become, she shucked out of her panties, parted her legs, and slipped a hand beneath her dress. Her fingers slid into her warm, wet entrance while she circled her thumb around her clit. With a moan, she closed her eyes, rested her head on the back of the chair, and —false leg braced against the floor—eased her other foot onto the desktop. That felt so good. A groan rumbled up her throat and past her lips. Her sexed-up brain conjured John, painted him into the office doorway watching her pleasure herself, while an erection tented his jeans. He moaned.

Wait.

Not her imagination.

Oh shit.

Her not-quite-a-son-in-law stood there, watching her finger fuck herself.

Carla froze, caught with her hand in the biscuit tin. No getting out of this one. Bare-chested, he eased fully into the room and pushed the door closed behind him. Then, thumbs hooked inside the waistband of his denims, he leant back and studied her.

The rounded ridges of his six-pack drew her eyes. Not to mention the man-mountain between his hands. Around each wrist, he wore black cord bracelet-type-things, and a matching black cord hung around his neck, from which dangled a small silver cross, which nestled in his chest hair. Muscles bulged everywhere, and a prominent vein through his biceps begged for her to lick it.

Dazed, Carla blinked, cleared her throat, and eased her fingers out from between her thighs. Freed, they exuded the smell of her sex into the small enclosed space.

John breathed in deep through his nose. Then, eyes locked on her, he said, 'Don't move.'

Carla gasped, sucked in a needy breath, and found she couldn't breathe out. From his place in front of the door, he stared, attention zeroed between her legs. She felt exposed and incredibly aroused at the same time. Carla liked that he looked at her with that much hunger in his smouldering brown eyes.

The atmosphere in the room thickened while the air between them shimmered with the heat of their fiery gazes. Carla daren't move, not even to blink, for fear of breaking the spell. Even though she hadn't quite made up her mind which way she wanted this to go yet.

'Let me help you with that, Mrs Thornton.'

'Ungh.'

A sweet, adorable, and utterly wicked smile stretched his lips and lit his eyes. Not letting her free from his gaze the whole way, he strolled across the room, edged around the desk, and stopped at her side. Perched on the corner of the table, he snagged her fun-hand and sucked her sex-stickied-fingers into his mouth. 'Mmm.' Once he'd licked her clean, he eased her hand to her lap and brushed his lips over hers. The faint taste of Carla's arousal lingered on his mouth. Oh God.

He pulled back so that his face hovered only an inch from hers, and said, 'What were you fantasising about?'

Carla blushed enough to tint the light in the room red. 'Ungh.'

John chuckled, leaned in for another taste of her lips, and then urged her, 'Come on. No need for shyness between friends. Was it me?' He licked his lips, and rubbed his abdomen with his knuckles as he slid his hands along his waistband. 'I've seen the way you look at me, Mrs Thornton. What sorts of things have I done to you?'

This close, she could smell his body. Smell his need. Juice squirted out of her. OMG. Carla groaned. '*John.*' That's all she could manage—that one, teeny, soft whisper.

John eased her foot to the floor, grasped either side of the chair, and spun it until she faced side-on to the table. Then he slid from the desktop and dropped to his knees between her legs, which she parted for him when he wriggled in for a kiss. This was no soft brush of lips, though. No, this time, he mashed his mouth against hers, and then thrust his tongue into her. Their teeth clacked together as he explored her roughly, and wrapped his tongue around her much smaller, softer one.

Calloused, hot hands rested on the insides of her knees while he explored her with his tongue. He thrust insistently, letting her know exactly what he'd like to do to her elsewhere, and rubbed his hands higher until they met her wetness. Carla groaned. Then, when he slipped a finger between her folds, she whimpered and gripped his shoulders.

His muscles rippled beneath her fingers, and she dug her nails in at the first invasion deeper into her core. He started with one finger, then slipped in a second, and then a third. With a deft twist, he rubbed his thumb over her clit. Carla's hips bucked against him, and he pressed his chest to hers. Rapid thumping vibrated through his pecs, showing Carla that he was at least as excited as she. Not knowing what else to do with him, she ran her hands up and down his back, and everywhere else she could reach.

Neck, back, chest, abs, … not *there,* though. Nope, she stopped at his waistband every time. Until he grabbed a hand and pushed it there. Man-mountain had she called it? He made her bunny look tiny. Oh. My. God. Carla rubbed him through the thick fabric, while he plundered her with his tongue and fingers. Her pulse raced, and sweat slicked her body while her breath came in short pants and gasps.

She was going to come. Right here, in this chair, with John—this impossibly young, hot guy—knelt between her legs, doing things to her. Magic things. Oh God. Her nerve endings zinged and pinged, and she rocked against his hand, frantic and overwhelmed with sensation. Foreplay with Eric had never even remotely resembled this. Then the landslide hit, and she was helpless but to tumble down with it. Her walls clenched tight around his fingers, and she cried out into his mouth as she came. Come like she hadn't come before.

He held her tight until she stopped cutting off the blood flow to his digits, then he eased out of her and pulled her into his chest. Wrapped in his warm embrace, while he nuzzled her neck, Carla drifted back down to Earth. John let her breathing slow before making her speak. In a voice of velvet, he asked, 'Is that what you were after?'

'Ooh, you're such a bad boy.' Robbed of her voice, Carla could still only manage a husky whisper.

John nibbled at her earlobe. 'Bad, huh? You ain't seen nothing yet, babe.'

She giggled and squirmed as he nibbled some more. 'No? What do you have planned next?' Carla hardly recognised the sexy, husky, breathy voice as her own.

He eased away and stared into her eyes while he rested her hand on his delightful bulge. His words alone nearly made her come again.

'First, I'm gonna slip into that tiny hot mouth of yours, and you're going to take everything I give you. Then I'm gonna fuck that slick, tight pussy until you beg me to stop. After that, we'll see what treasures you've got hidden behind your back door.'

Just in case she hadn't taken him seriously enough, he claimed her mouth once more and invaded her with his tongue. If Carla got any wetter, she'd end up having to replace her chair. It must be drenched by now.

John wrapped his hands around her and slid his hands beneath her buttocks. Then he grabbed her and rose to his feet. She wrapped her legs around his hips, and he carried her to the desk, and when he sat on the edge, she slid down him until she knelt astride his lap. He squeezed her buttocks and tongued her some more. His erection pushed at his jeans, and the stiff zipper-seam rubbed against her exposed pussy when she rocked against him.

Then the hard ridge of her prosthetic leg pressed painfully

against her stump. She lifted off him and said, 'Just a sec.'

John let her go and helped her shift position without losing her balance. Seated on the desk next to him, she reached down to the middle of the socket and pressed the lock release button. With a whoosh as the suction released, the limb slipped from the end of her leg. Carla rested it against the table drawers, and then leaned into John as he wrapped an arm around her.

'That's better,' she murmured.

'Does it hurt?' Concern clouded his eyes.

People rarely asked her about it, and when they took the trouble, Carla felt that careful honesty was always the best policy. With a shrug, she said, 'Most of the time.' She gave him a smile. 'It's okay, though—I'm used to it.' Then she tilted her chin up for a kiss, and John obliged.

Carla manoeuvred until she once again straddled him, and the posture felt much easier free of the prosthesis. Should she confess that she'd not done this with anyone since the accident? If she did, he'd work out that she hadn't had sex in ten years. How embarrassing would that be?

The fact that every other amputee she knew, or had heard of, managed much better than she did, remained a source of chagrin and shame. Even though she knew that the nerve damage had simply been too severe for her to achieve normal mobility with the false limb, everyone else didn't. Carla caught it in their looks, and felt judged and inadequate. When other amputees hiked through the Arctic, played sports, and even sprinted in the Olympics, why did she need sticks to get around for anything more than pottering around the house? How come she couldn't stay on her feet long without ending up in severe pain? What was wrong with her? Didn't she want to be normal?

Attentive, John picked up on her downer. 'You okay?' He pecked her on the cheek and watched her expression carefully.

Carla buried her face in his neck before she could bring herself to continue with the honesty. 'I haven't done this … been with anyone … since I lost the leg. And, I'm not as good as other amputees. I … it just …'

John hooked a finger under her chin and nudged her until she looked up at him. 'You're perfect. I wanted you the second I set eyes on you.'

'But, I'm old …'

He rolled his eyes but with a grin. 'From where I'm sitting, that doesn't seem to be making any difference.' He rubbed his hardness against her and nibbled at her bottom lip. Then he grabbed her bottom and squeezed. 'I always did prefer whisky.'

Carla chuckled, despite her misgivings. 'Whisky?'

John kissed her, and then said, 'Mature. Hot as hell. Burns when it goes down.'

For the gazillionth time that day, Carla gasped. Embarrassed and delighted, she buried her face into the crook of his neck. Then nuzzled him with her lips. He tasted good. Her tongue flicked out and licked at his collarbone. Then she traced the vein down his arm, stopping at the crook of his elbow and nibbling some more.

John let out a low half-moan, half-growl and kissed the top of her head. Carla pushed at his chest until he got the message and lay back, toned body sprawled across her expansive work desk. After giving his ripped abs an appreciative glance, Carla kissed her way down his torso. John twigged what she was up to and shuffled further onto the table so she could go lower without falling off the edge.

When she got to his waistband, she teased her tongue around his navel and hooked her fingers beneath the fabric. His muscles bunched up beneath her touch, and he ran his hands through her short hair. He'd said he wanted to slip into her mouth … *her tiny hot mouth* … and it sounded so damn sexy, but she'd never done that before.

Carla slid his zip down and unfastened the button. He bulged through the opening she'd made, and she took hold of him and freed him from his boxers. John groaned and circled his hips. Carla hesitated. Glanced along his length until she met his gaze. His lowered lids told her he'd been laying there and watching her. Did he want to look at her while she took him into her mouth? The thought shot heat and excitement through her.

'Don't do anything you're not comfortable with,' he said. 'And, if you don't like something that I do, you have to tell me.

Deal?'

Relieved, Carla nodded. 'I want to give it a try.' She nodded toward his engorged cock.

'But you don't know if it's for you?'

Another nod. She tried to ignore the bit of her that felt mortified that she needed to have this conversation at forty-three years of age. He wasn't like she'd expected. A guy as hot as him could take his pick of women, and yet here he was, with her, being so gentle and patient. Carla swallowed a surge of emotion when he sat up and pulled her in for a tender kiss.

'Want to stop?'

She shook her head. 'No chance.' And felt better when she managed a chuckle. If not for his obvious arousal, she might have worried she'd just murdered the moment. Wanting to recapture it for herself, she kissed him back with more pressure and insistence while reaching for his member.

Pre-cum beaded on the end and slicked her fingers when she worked up and down his length and rubbed her thumb over the head. Beneath her, John moaned and thrust his hungry tongue into her mouth. His hands found her breasts. He broke the kiss to pull her dress over her head. Her nipples pebbled as she knelt on the hard wood, naked. John did a sit up so he could suck a nipple into his mouth, and then he nibbled it, and lapped with his tongue. Lightning struck. Shot straight from her tits to her clit.

Eager now, Carla eased him onto his back and turned her attention to his lower half. With a bit of help from him, she got rid of his jeans and boxers, and then took firm hold of him. First, she ran her tongue up and down his shaft, then licked across the slit, and sucked him into her mouth.

His girth proved enough to stretch her lips and make her feel full, and long enough that if she took him all the way in, he'd hit the back of her throat. She started slow and shallow, and worked him in and out of her, gradually increasing the tempo and penetration. His pre-cum tasted slightly salty and musky. Nice. Carla hadn't expected that pleasuring him like this would also pleasure her. It excited her, having him in her mouth, thrusting and groaning as her tongue sucked and licked. Faster and faster, harder and harder she went, until his abdomen clenched and he grabbed either side of her head. With a gentle grip, he eased her up and off him. Carla knelt there, panting and wet and ready.

'Unless you want me to come right now, you'd better stop.'

Then he pulled her down so she lay on top of him and kissed her. 'I know where I'd rather come,' he said with a grin and another kiss. His erection pressed into her belly, and his thigh rubbed between her soaked folds.

It was too much. She needed him inside her. Filling her. Carla wriggled until her legs lay either side of his firm hips, then she reached between their slick bodies and took hold of him until he lay at her entrance. John grabbed her round the waist and then pushed into her. Bliss filled her as she slid down his thick length.

She came straight away, as soon as his balls pushed against her buttocks and the base of his cock rubbed against her clit. He held onto her as she writhed and bucked and gasped on top of him. His hard heat inside her felt so damn good.

When her shudders eased, John flipped her onto her back and covered her. With a firm stroke, he thrust into her. All the way in. Oh God. Then he hooked her knees over his shoulders, which parted her even further and allowed him deeper access. Carla whimpered and clawed at his back as he took her, arms braced either side of her head on the desktop. Her slick walls clenched around him while excitement built until she felt sure she would die from the pleasure. He fucked her, hard and fast, and she came again. Waves of heat rolled through her, and her muscles spasmed around him—milking him. He increased the tempo of his thrusts and buried his mouth at the base of her neck. Then he grunted and stiffened against her. His cock pulsed inside her, and he filled her with his cum.

Spent, he lay over her, panting and nuzzling. When he softened, he lifted away from her and pulled her to the edge of the desk when he stood. Then he picked her up and carried her to the chair, where he sat down with her nestled in his lap. Carla's whole body sang when he wrapped his solid arms around her and pulled her into his warm, firm chest, peppering her with kisses the whole while.

They both jumped and froze at the distant shout of, 'Mom?'

With a nervous giggle, Carla grabbed her prosthetic leg and stood up as she shoved her stump into the socket. It clicked like some kind of deranged cricket as she ratcheted the pin into the lock. Clicked and locked, she cast a panicked glance around until she located her dress, crumpled on the far side of the desk. With another nervous giggle, Carla lunged for it and pulled it hurriedly over her head.

A quick look at John showed that he'd managed to pull on his boxers, but only had one foot in the top of his jeans. Not quick enough by a long shot. Only one thing for it. She headed for the door, to stop her daughter before she could burst into the office and find them like this. Before she pulled it open, she caught John's eye. He grinned and winked and mouthed, 'Later.' Carla smoothed her hair down, swallowed, and took a fortifying breath before venturing into the hallway. She had to suck her cheeks in hard to wipe the silly grin from her face.

Emma watched her from the kitchen doorway, eyes narrowed in suspicion. 'Where did you get to? I thought you were going for drinks.'

Carla moved toward her, so the young woman had to back up and edge into the kitchen. 'Sorry. A call came in, and then things … got on top of me.'

Emma peered at her mother in the bright light of the kitchen. 'Are you okay? You're all flushed.'

Carla made a show of exasperation and raised her hands in the air. 'It's hot. What do you expect? Come on, you can give me a hand. Grab the glasses, will you?'

Emma gave her a long look, but then did as asked.

Then Jake meandered in and asked, 'Where's John got to?'

Carla almost choked. Resolutely staring at the fridge while she pressed a tumbler against the switch that would trigger the ice-dispenser, and all innocence, she said, 'Oh? Is he not out there with you?'

Jake shook his head, hands on hips, glancing around the room, as if John might be hiding under one of the counters. 'Nope. He came in ages ago.'

Carla had to stifle a wild giggle. He certainly had come in. She cleared her throat and said, 'Um, maybe he went to the bathroom or something?'

Right on cue, John sauntered in, looking all cute and gorgeous and sexy and … Get. A. Grip. Carla grabbed the next glass and proceeded to dump ice in it, pretending a total lack of interest when—in reality—her every sense went into hyperdrive as he stepped past her to head for the patio doors.

To his brother, he said, 'Sorry, mate. Had to take a dump. You know how it gets sometimes when—'

'Guys are so gross,' Emma said, screwing up her face.

Something thick and sticky dribbled down Carla's leg. Oh God. No.

Sadly, yes. It so was.

Ashen-faced, she shoved the tumbler at Emma and squeaked, 'Erm, speaking of which, your mother needs the bathroom. Excuse me.' Then she made a run for it—well, as much as she could with the damn leg—all the while praying that she didn't leave any *evidence* behind. She managed to hold in the fit of giggles until she dived into the bathroom and locked the door behind her.

OMG Carla Thornton. What. Did. You. Just. *Do*?

Not until she lifted her dress up did she miss her knickers. Where the hell were they? Then she lost it. Proper lost it. She had to shove her fist in her mouth to muffle her loud guffaws, and the tears streamed down her beetroot face.

Hil—air—rious.

And so what if Emma sussed it out? They were both grown adults. Consenting adults. Just because she was old enough to be his mother. That was so yesterday's news.

Yep, maybe if she kept on long enough, she'd convince herself, but so far, it wasn't working so well. Fun as it had been, she couldn't go there again. It was wrong. So very wrong. And, OMG, she'd never liked being wrong so much.

Yeah, maybe she *could* do a replay after all.

When Carla finally felt steady enough to leave the bathroom, she detoured to the office in search of certain lost property, but her lace panties were nowhere to be found. Damn. What had the man done with them? Lips pursed, she made her way to the kitchen, which now stood empty. Voices drifted in from outside. Looked like they'd taken the drinks out there with them.

From the laundry basket, full of ironing to do, Carla snagged a fresh pair of knickers. Then, shoulders squared, spine set, and just-had-my-brains-shagged-out-grin firmly smothered, she followed the laughter and banter.

Outside, Jake and Emma lay sprawled on a blanket in the middle of the lawn. John sat at the eight-person patio table, sipping from a can of lager. Beads of moisture had collected on the tin, as the cool container met the blast-furnace heat of the afternoon. Idly, he ran a finger through the condensation. Carla found that incredibly erotic for some reason.

Nervous as a virgin, Carla dragged her feet toward the patio set. And John. He raised his eyebrows above a cheeky grin when she approached. In spite of her misgivings, Carla smiled and winked. Then she picked up the tumbler of gin and bitter lemon waiting for her on the table top. The ice had melted already. Yep, her flushed cheeks were *so* down to the heat of the day.

Torn, wanting to simultaneously jump into his lap and stay as far away from him as possible, Carla chose a chair a couple of places down the table from him. The shade from the parasol felt awesome. The sudden loss of the sun was the sole reason for the goosebumps that erupted up her arms. It had nothing whatsoever to do with the fact that John had just rolled the can across his chest and licked his lips while looking right at her.

Carla stuck out her tongue in retaliation. A mistake. He mimed sucking on it, and it was all she could do to sit still and not laugh out loud or pounce on him.

The afternoon dragged on, and by six o'clock, Carla felt desperate. Then she had the brainwave of sending Emma and Jake out for a pizza takeaway. It would take them at least an hour. Loads of time. The masterful plan nearly backfired when Jake asked John if he wanted to go with. Carla held her breath. Held everything tight, in fact. John stretched like a cat drowsing on a hot bonnet, and said, 'Nah. If you don't mind, I'll stay put. Dunno why, but I'm knackered.' He shot Carla the look of a devil. She could have slapped him.

Oh, the relief when Jake smiled and told his brother, 'No worries, mate.'

Emma caught her mother's eye and said, 'We won't be long.'

'No hurry,' Carla told them.

The slam of the front door shutting behind Emma and Jake rumbled through the house and reached John and Carla in the back garden. With a mischievous glint in his eyes, he reached into his pocket and pulled out something lacy.

'You missing these?'

'You sod.'

He grinned, swirled them around his finger. Then they pounced on one another. On their feet, John clamped his mouth down on hers and shoved his tongue past her waiting lips. His hands roamed everywhere. Carla pulled away and, with one hand she grabbed her panties, and with the other took hold of his palm. 'You too tired then?' she asked him with a grin, and tugged him toward the house.

'Yeah. Reckon I need to go and lie down.' They shared a giggle as she pulled him through the kitchen and into the hallway.

Carla fully intended to take him upstairs to her room, but they never made it past the middle of the stairs. Halfway up, with Carla one step above him, he took hold of her waist from behind and pulled her into him. His erect penis pushed into her buttocks, and he lowered his head and nibbled at her ear while fondling her breasts. Then he reached a hand beneath her dress and slipped it into her no-longer-so-fresh knickers. Carla moaned at the pleasure when he parted her wet folds and delved into her slick entrance. He worked his fingers in and out of her and nipped at her clit.

Carla reached behind him to grab his firm buttocks and pull his groin further into her. Then she tilted her head back and twisted a little so he could plant his lips on hers. His tongue probed and licked, and his taste and scent drove her wild.

Unable to wait any longer, needing him inside her right then, she fumbled with his zip and shoved his jeans down his legs as far as she could reach from this awkward position.

John let her go long enough to shove his pants down to his knees, and then he yanked her dress over her head for the second time that day. Next to go were her knickers. Then he shoved her forward, so she fell onto hands and knees on the stairs. From behind, he rubbed the side of his hand between her folds and over her clit. Carla bucked and whimpered. 'John. Please. Now.'

'Say it.' He rubbed her again, with more pressure. 'What do you want?'

'Oh God, John. Fuck me. Now. Please.'

He groaned into her mouth, and then reached between them and took hold of himself. She felt him stroke the shaft a couple of times, then he positioned his cock at her entrance and shoved into her. Hot and hard and engorged, he filled her. His balls slapped at her buttocks when he thrust his full length into her, and she arched her back with a cry of ecstasy. He grabbed her breasts and squeezed, teasing the nipples as he took her over and over. He penetrated her again and again with hot animal passion, grunting as his need to come built.

Carla felt delirious, desperate to orgasm. Each thrust brought exquisite torture that she wanted to last forever and also couldn't bear for another moment. Her need climbed to a frenzy, and she clenched around him. 'Oh, John. Yes.'

He gripped her hips and pounded into her as deep as she could take. Then he bit her shoulder. 'John!' she yelled on the crest of the wave, and then whimpered when her orgasm broke and crashed to shore. He filled her even more when her walls clenched around him, and then he bit her again and jerked while he spilled inside her. 'Fuck, baby.'

Then he kissed the bites, and nuzzled into her neck. 'What did you do to me, woman?'

Panting, slick with perspiration, and satiated, Carla collapsed to her stomach with a giggle. John kissed her shoulders and shuffled them around until he sat on a stair and pulled her into his lap.

Carla's heart squeezed with joy when he said, 'Be with me. No more hiding. Let me get old with you.'

CHAPTER SEVEN

Night Nurse

Denise raised a pale hand to her bare head as she stared at her ghostly reflection in the dresser mirror. The chemo had done its worst and left her utterly ravaged. Gone were her waist-length golden locks, her rounded rosy cheeks, and that special spark of life behind her blue eyes—dulled now, and flat. Gone too, was Geoff. So much for *until death do us part ... in sickness and in health,* and all the rest of that rubbish. And really, with only weeks left to live, she didn't need the complication or aggravation. Much better going it alone.

Next, her gaze travelled down her lined face to her pencil-thin neck, and further still to the ruins of what used to be a full-bosomed chest. She nudged her cotton nightie aside and studied the surgeon's work—he'd made a good job of a bad situation.

They'd offered her fake boobs to wear and wigs, but such subterfuge went wholly against who she was. Honesty and accepting things as they were had been her lifelong motto. Why change things now? Why go for uncomfortable compromise just to make others feel easier? Especially with so little time left.

With that kind of constraint, those limitations on life, the small stuff needed to be sweated over. It mattered. It's the tiny, inconsequential stuff that builds a life, after all. Even though we only tend to notice the big things, the wow moments, the stuff of dreams, that's not what fills most of our waking hours.

Rather, the burst of sun through a break in heavy clouds, the smell of that first summer rose or freshly cut grass, the robin's gift of crimson in a denuded, brown winter garden, or the first time your baby looks you in the eyes and smiles.

When she turned thirty, Denise had all those things. Her thirty-fifth birthday had dawned this morning without any noticeable sunrise to lift the blackness in her heart. No husband, no little Susie, and not even a home to call her own. So, there she sat, staring into the mirror because that had to be better than staring into the abyss that had swallowed her soul. A void full of the awful emptiness in the question, *what fills your life right now?*

What constitutes life? What fills the yawning hours of empty days? Who are you once the chemo and the cancer have stripped you bare? Perhaps, most importantly of all, did she plan to go out on a slow fizzle or with a big bang? Did she even have any choice? Right then, it seemed as though the universe had taken any and all free will from her, along with everything else.

From the living room, the murmur of hushed voices swapping information about her reached Denise's ears. Sally, the Macmillan nurse who'd spent the afternoon with her, was busy handing over to Ian, who would do a sleepover in case she needed anything in the night. Maureen would take over in the morning. Such names marked the last hours of her freedom. The last precious moments before an ambulance would come to take her to the hospice.

Denise brightened when she heard the front door close and Ian's footsteps in the hallway. Of all her carers, she'd grown closest to him. Her illness had seen her become a vampire—sleeping in the day, pale, and utterly bloodless. Perforce, he'd been her main company through the graveyard hours. By choice, he'd fallen into the habit of sitting with her even on his off days.

At first, she'd resented his generosity; rejected what she took as pity. It took some convincing that he wanted to be her friend. And then, of course, she'd swung all the way to the other side of the spectrum. Wanted more than he felt able to give. It seemed all he did intend was friends. Silly woman; ought to have known he wouldn't be interested in her in *that* way. Who would? Hairless, breastless, restless, and almost bloodless. Not yet lifeless, though. Not yet.

A wry smile tugged at her mouth, strange in its rarity. She used to smile all the time, and laugh. Not any more. Even this small, brief smile held more irony than happy. Ian obviously liked her for her sparkling personality. Once upon a time, it could have held a physical promise. Once upon a time … no chance of a happily ever after.

Her bedroom door edged open, and Ian's sweet, smiling face peered in. He found her eyes. 'Hey, D. You ready for bed?'

Sally had helped her into her nightie, but as exhausted as she felt, she wasn't the least bit sleepy. Denise shook her head. Sighed. 'Read to me?'

Ian nodded and smiled wider. These days, she didn't have the energy or the concentration to read for herself. She just couldn't focus. What she could do, was lay there with closed eyes and open ears, letting his melodic tenor make magic in her mind.

Initially, she'd let him choose the books, and kept her penchant for erotic romance firmly hidden. What business did a dead woman have looking for sexual excitement? But she did, damn it. Denise still had a pulse—weak, but definitely there. Just because she couldn't do much about it, didn't mean she couldn't think about it. More irony—even after everything and with nothing, she still had her dreams, her fantasies.

The recent misunderstanding between Ian and she had helped—the clichéd silver lining. While her attempt to kiss him had resulted in mortifying awkwardness for them both, it had alerted him to certain needs that her otherwise excellent care package had failed to provide for. Despite not having the energy for physical arousal, she still had plenty of brain power. Never would she have considered how rewarding mental stimulation could be.

Ian, more in tune with her each night, had been the one to ask about erotica. Through a furious flush, Denise had admitted that she'd prefer him to read that kind of book instead. And so it had begun. With Ian's help, Denise got into bed and snuggled beneath the heavy winter duvet, in spite of the warmth of the room. Another side effect—always being cold.

After a couple of weeks of routine, Ian managed to read without stuttering and stammering his way through the hot bits. Didn't even pause at the odd moan that might escape relaxed lips. For Denise's part, she would lay there with eyes shut and let his words wash through her. All the while, her brain would superimpose her and Ian over whoever the main characters were supposed to be. It would be his hands caressing her, his lips crushing hers, and his tongue plundering her needy mouth. Surprisingly, given her excited state, she could often fall asleep this way. At such times, her sleep would be filled with heat and pleasure, rather than pain and unease.

Ian settled into the armchair pulled close to the side of the bed. As had become their routine, he balanced the book in one hand and took hold of hers in the other. Denise admired his skill at turning the pages without needing to let go of her. He'd grip the book in two fingers while flipping the page with his thumb. Best of all, he'd learned that just for her.

Denise lay in bed and watched him. While not a stunner, he had a certain male prettiness about him. At forty, he still looked fairly trim with only a hint of a possible paunch. He wore his hair loosely cropped, which showed off his thick black waves perfectly. An old break had left him with a crooked nose, which added to his cuteness. Then there were his eyes. Those dark brown orbs had captured her from the instant she met him.

Whether he showed up in his nurse's uniform, or his jeans and tee, he wore them well and looked good. Although, Denise had to admit, his regular clothes hugged his figure in a rather alluring way. The times she'd rested her gaze on the stiff denim at his crotch and imagined pulling the zip down with her teeth.

Tonight, his uniform was absent. A wave of desire left her flushed and perspiring.

In need of distraction while she waited for him to find his place in the book and sort himself out, Denise let her mind drift to the night of their misunderstanding. When she'd pressed her lips to his, he'd returned the pressure but kept it chaste. Had let her down gently. Explained that he would lose his job if he made it personal with her. Four weeks later, she wondered—still—if he would have, if not for his professional constraints. A week after the letdown, he'd begun to read the daring stuff, and a few nights later had taken her hand and held onto it.

Maybe he was softening toward her? More like wishful thinking. She had to be careful not to read too much into small gestures. Denise shook her head and bit her cheek. As much as she wanted something to happen on her last night pre-hospice, she had to keep it real. Early in life, she'd learned the pain of the blade hidden within the velvet glove of fooling oneself. Far better to recognise and acknowledge the knife for what it was, in all its cold, hard, sharp steel. Velvet and silk were no good unless they were so soft and true all the way through. If you knew it was there, could see it, you could prepare for it. Letting things catch you by surprise was when you were most likely to get cut. Geoff had been sharp steel pretending to be velvet. Not until he'd taken Susie and her home did Denise have any inkling she was so vulnerable.

Book in a firm grip, Ian took her hand and cleared his throat, pulling her out of her head. She lived in her mind far too much these days. Denise glanced at him, and he asked, 'Ready?'

A quick nod, then she closed her eyes and waited. At about a third of the way into the story, the tension had mounted, and Denise felt eager anticipation at what tonight's chapters would hold. Surely the author had to give it up now? Ian's soft tones chased away her last errant thoughts, '*Louise slammed the trunk shut. Firm arms took her from behind. One at her waist, another across her breasts. Something hard nudged at the small of her back, and Louise had no trouble identifying what that might be. Calloused hands, used to heavier work than this, slipped into the open neck of her blouse and squeezed her breasts. Hot lips nuzzled at her neck, while finger and thumb rolled her nipple, which pebbled at the touch. A heavy tug had her jeans button undone and her zip down. …'*

Denise's brain filled in the essentials … Ian's hot smooth hand plunged into the waistband of her panties and down between her legs, while his other hand reached into her blouse and squeezed her breasts. Heat and desire filled her, and when he rolled a nipple between thumb and forefinger, wetness drenched her panties. He parted her folds and slipped a finger into her. 'Oh fuck, baby, you're so hot and wet for me.' He nipped at the tender, sensitive place between shoulder and neck.

Then he tugged at her clothes, until her jeans and knickers wrapped around her calves. Seconds later, she felt his hard cock pressing at her slick entrance, and then he thrust into her.

She cried out, 'Ian!'

He stopped reading. Denise snapped open her eyes. Heat flooded her face. She'd said that out loud, hadn't she? A look at his expression confirmed her fears. In the squeakiest voice ever, she said, 'Sorry.' No amount of deep breathing settled her racing pulse or her humiliation. 'Oh shit.'

Beside the bed, Ian closed the book and set it on the bedside table. A few seconds passed in thick silence, punctuated by Denise's pulse hammering in her ears. And then Ian said, 'We need to talk.' The squeeze he gave her hand helped some, but she couldn't meet his eyes. Instead, she nodded and said, 'I really am sorry.'

In a quiet voice, he told her, 'You don't have to be.'

'I embarrassed us both, again. I know how you feel.'

He cleared his throat a second time and shifted in the chair. 'Well, actually, you don't.'

Denise did look at him then. Surprise and curiosity nudged her chagrin into a dark corner and took centre stage. Ian held her gaze and took both her hands in his, which had him leaning forward and close enough for her to feel his breath on her cheek and smell the coffee he'd drunk earlier.

When she could no longer bear the quiet, the waiting, she

nudged him, 'What don't I know?' Her voice had gone from squeaky to husky.

'I handed in my notice.'

'What?'

'Tonight isn't just my night off. It's my first night here as nothing more than a concerned friend.'

'A concerned friend?' She could barely breathe. Desperate for more of an explanation, Denise sucked in air and asked, 'Ian? Why would you?'

His thumb rubbed the back of her hand while he sat and stared into her eyes—into her soul by the feel of it. She saw the moment he made his decision. 'That night when you tried to kiss me …'

No longer just bloodless or breathless, but wordless too, Denise could only lay and watch him.

'I wanted you so badly,' he said at a near whisper, voice as hoarse as Denise's had been.

A soft sob freed itself and brought her words with it. 'You never said.'

'I couldn't. Not until I wasn't your nurse any more. And now I've left it too late.'

Denise wriggled one of her hands loose and reached up to hold the back of his head and pull him down to her. The kiss started tentative—barely there, and gradually built in intensity and passion. Then she nudged at his lips with her tongue, and he opened for her. He felt so soft, and tasted rich and satisfying like dark chocolate and red wine. When he eased a hand to the back of her head and held it, Denise stiffened. The complete lack of hair made the touch much more intimate, but also reminded her of how she looked.

Ian paused and pulled back to regard her. Inside her head, as ever, he said, 'You're beautiful.' He stopped and shook his head. 'That's not important. What I want to say is that you're so much more than how you look or what you wear … you're intelligent, funny, honest, passionate, so brave—'

'Stop, will you.' Denise grinned and blushed.

Ian laughed and said, 'And modest …'

Denise swatted him on the chest. With a look of love and

longing in his eyes, Ian leant in and kissed her. 'I've grown to love you, not just admire you.'

'Oh, Ian.'

It quickly grew uncomfortable trying to hug one another in that position, so—with Ian's help—Denise shuffled to the other side of the bed and patted the mattress. Ian climbed atop the duvet and worked his arm beneath her neck, and she ended up laying with her head resting on his chest and his arms around her. Bed covers between them.

Ian rested his chin on the top of her head while his hands stroked her skin wherever he could reach without disturbing her cosy cocoon—hands, arms, cheeks. Denise relaxed more completely than she could remember ever doing. Here was a man who had gotten to know her at the worst time of her life, had seen her at her lowest, and loved her for it—for who she was, not some image of who he thought she was or should be. All at once, she'd gone from being empty and hollow to being full and complete. Overflowing.

In that open state, more of his earlier words filtered through … *I've left it too late.* Denise pulled one of his hands to her mouth and kissed the back of it. 'While we have life, it's never too late.'

Beneath her, Ian's breathing stilled for a beat or two, and then he said, 'You're going into the hospice tomorrow.'

Denise played with his fingers. 'I don't have to. I can delay the admission.'

'No, Denise, I'd never ask you to do that.'

Her first real happy smile in months stretched her lips, lifted her cheeks, and lit her eyes. 'Let me rephrase that. I *want* to delay it.'

Again with the falling silent. They seemed to be doing so much of their communicating without words. Whether it be heavy and full of tension, or light, loving, and full of acceptance—their lack of vocalising spoke volumes.

Without anything verbal passing between them, Denise knew without a doubt that Ian had soaked in her words and wishes. And, because of this, she wasn't at all surprised when he did use his words.

'Marry me.'

'No.' She grinned.

'No?' His tone told her he'd heard her smile. As did the kiss he dropped onto her naked skull.

'It's a leap year. You marry me.'

Ian mock-sighed. 'Okay. I suppose so.'

Denise swatted at his chest again, then eased round so they could kiss. The fact that it took her so much longer than it should just made it all the sweeter and more poignant. Something to savour. Like her next breath, nothing could be taken for granted. It all had to be noticed and appreciated. Every teeny tiny thing. How blessed she was to have been so abandoned by her past, and having any future snuffed out—it left her firmly in the present, in all its vivid pain and delight.

The divorce had done her a favour, once she'd gotten over the shock and feelings of betrayal and hurt. Geoff's actions had taken away the worry of what her girl would do when she was gone. Had removed the necessity of fussing over silly things like mortgages and house deeds and leaving behind distraught loved ones. Then Denise caught herself and giggled. Hadn't she just agreed to tie her and Ian together in that self-same way?

No. The answer came so clearly and forcefully that its truth settled into her marrow. Ian was like sugar to Geoff's salt. They might look the same, but woe betide you if you put the wrong one in your coffee.

Case in point … Ian didn't need to ask her what her little giggle had been for, but was happy at her happy. His only response was to snuggle into her further and give a contented sigh. Where had he been all her life? And how lucky was she to have found him? How many people lived and died without ever meeting their soul mate? No, with this man, she wouldn't be leaving any grieving husband behind. They would live a love so full and complete that there could never be any room for even an ounce of regret. The kind of love that existed outside of time and space. The kind of love that would give them a lifetime instead of mere weeks.

At least, that was all enough for Denise. She'd best check. 'Are you scared?' she asked.

'No.' His answer came back strong and confident. 'I only felt scared that I wouldn't say anything before I lost you.' He paused for a couple of seconds, and then proved yet again how much they shared a single wavelength. 'Not that I'll be losing you. From here on in, I can only gain.'

They kissed deeply—making a promise more profound than any wedding ceremony could ever give. A wave of joy engulfed Denise and turned her to jelly. Or did the trembling come from another sensation? She'd settle for it being both. As the wave ebbed, another one carrying exhaustion rolled in and pulled her eyes closed. She fell asleep even while her lips still rested on his.

The next morning, Ian tried to ease from the bed without waking her, but she roused as soon as he slipped his hand from beneath her neck. He kissed her thoroughly, then said, 'Morning, sleepy head.'

'Mmm, that has to be the best I've slept in forever.'

Ian smiled and gave her another kiss. 'I'll have to come and be your sleeping pill tonight then.'

Denise made a decision. 'Come here, not to Saint Catherine's.'

Ian raised his eyebrows. 'You sure? I can marry you in the hospice as well as I can here.'

'I know. I want to push it back a week. We'll manage.'

He squeezed her hand. 'What can I do?'

'See how soon a minister can come here and marry us.'

'On it. Want me to call anyone?'

'Nah. If you want anybody to come, just go ahead and sort it out, but I've already said all my goodbyes, and I don't want to open the wounds back up for my friends. We'll tell them after the event.'

Ian smiled. 'If I know you at all, I'd bet on you already having your final words written out.'

A quiet knock sounded at the front door and then it clicked open, letting in the noise of the traffic along with Maureen. Ian planted a quick kiss on Denise's lips, told her, 'later,' and headed into the hallway to go meet the morning nurse.

Wanting to stay awake as late as she could that night, Denise made sure to get as much shut-eye as she could, which—despite her sound sleep last night—proved easy, helped along by her morphine drip. Before Denise settled down for the day, she asked Maureen to make sure to get Sally to wake her at five-ish so she could make an effort for Ian.

As it happened, Denise woke on her own at three after four. In the mood for a small cup of coffee, she rang her bedside bell and asked Sally if she could make her a brew. The nurse smiled and bustled off to take care of it. When she returned, she brought a mug for herself and sat with Denise making small talk while they supped. Although Denise couldn't manage much of it, just the heat and the smell were a treat.

When they'd done, she enlisted the nurse's help in freshening up with a bed bath and undertaking the tiring job of putting on a dress. The nurse picked out a pale pink mock-wrap with a gentle flower pattern. Sally was great, and enthused about Ian the whole time. He'd told his colleagues what was up and they supported him fully. The nurse repeated frequently how thrilled she was for them both.

Denise needed a half-hour's rest before she could cope with taking care of her makeup. Even with help, these small tasks felt as draining as climbing Skiddaw had done a few years ago. She hadn't trained nearly hard enough to tackle that hill, but then she'd always loved walking and had assumed she could just take it in her stride. Needless to say, it'd taken her a couple of days to recover from that hike, but the exhilaration at the top had been so worth it.

Once they were done, Denise had another nap, and Sally woke her a few minutes before Ian was due to arrive so she could touch up her make up if she needed to. Not having hair to bother about relieved her—another first. Maybe the saying was true, and every cloud did have a silver lining. Perhaps people just didn't always know how to look for it. Living with cancer and facing death had changed the way Denise saw a lot of things. What had seemed so gargantuan in the past didn't even make a blip on the radar these days.

When the knock came, and the front door opened, Sally

hustled into the hallway and left Denise's heart racing in anticipation. The usual murmur of low voices ensued, and then Ian came into the room. He pulled up short when he saw her, wide-eyed and mouth forming an 'O'. Then a huge smile made it into a 'U' instead, and he strode to the bed, dropped his holdall to the floor, and wrapped his arms around her. He smelled of fresh air and frost. In the distance, Sally exited the house without intruding.

Ian pulled out of the kiss and removed his jacket and shoes. Then he eased onto the bed next to her, both of them on top of the covers. Denise couldn't wait to hear how he'd gotten on. 'Well?'

With a chuckle, he said, 'I spoke to the chaplain at Saint Catherine's, and he called a friendly minister. He can come the day after tomorrow.'

'Witnesses?'

'Are you serious? The whole team wants to come watch. We're gonna have to rearrange the furniture to get 'em all in. You're a popular gal, you know.'

Overwhelmed, full of emotion, Denise had to blink to keep the tears imprisoned behind her lashes. Ian leant in and pressed his lips to hers. Then he asked, 'You want to read tonight?'

Denise grinned. 'Nope. No more pretending. I've got myself a real, in-the-flesh male here.'

Concern flashed across his face—there then gone.

Denise's smile broadened. 'I can't make any promises about falling asleep on you, though, hot as you are.'

Ian's chuckle came out low and throaty and sexy. 'Can't think of a nicer way to fall asleep.' Then his lips found hers, and Denise got lost for a while.

Long dormant nerve endings came to life and zinged and tingled. Her heart thumped at her ribs while butterflies played in her belly. And all he'd done so far was give her a thorough kissing while stroking her arms. Then his lips wandered along her jawline and down to her neck, found the sensitive spot just behind her earlobe, and sucked and nipped. Denise moaned and fisted her hand in his thick hair.

Ian's hands wandered to her waist, her hips, down to her

thighs, and finally cupped her buttocks. He moved over her, holding most of his weight on his arms, but still his growing arousal made itself known. Beneath him, lost in a flood of sensation, Denise rolled her hips into his, and he moaned into the soft flesh at the nape of her neck. Then his lips lifted to hers again, and he lapped at her with his tongue.

Need filled her while she grew slick with an ache of longing. Ian reached beneath the hem of her dress and trailed his hand along her thigh, coming to rest at her panties, where he cupped her damp crotch. His breathing rasped nearly as badly as hers, and his erection grew fully hard and dug into her hip. Denise reached a hand down between them and took hold of him through his jeans, with the stiff fabric making a hard ridge over his bulge.

Ian nibbled at her bottom lip, then sucked on it and explored her mouth with his tongue. Denise massaged him, and with a low groan, he shoved the wet fabric of her panties to one side and slipped a finger between her slick folds. 'Oh, Ian,' she said with a gasp. For answer, he plundered her deeper with his tongue and slid his finger into her, slightly bent so it caught her g-spot as he rubbed it back and forth.

White-hot lightning streaked through her and she writhed beneath him, rocking her hips in time with his caresses. Ian rocked with her, against her hand at his groin, all the while destroying her senses with his tongue. Soft little moans and whimpers escaped Denise with each penetration of his finger and thrust of his hips. Cupped in her hand, his cock twitched, and the heat of him reached her through the denim.

Denise unfastened his button and tugged down his zip, then reached inside his boxers and pulled him free. He gave a gruff, short cry when she wrapped her hand around his hot, hard shaft and stroked down from tip to base.

She wanted flesh on flesh, and let go of him to shove his jeans and underwear down to his thighs. Ian pushed her dress up to her waist while continuing to fuck her with his finger. Denise grabbed his naked buttocks, which felt wonderfully firm under her soft hands. Then, keeping one hand at his arse, she took hold of him again and fisted her hand around his cock.

Their rhythm increased in tempo, and both of them gasped and moaned as they brought each other to the brink. His wiry pubic hair rubbed against the smooth flesh stretched over her hip bone, and tickled at her fingers. Denise's complete lack of body hair increased the feel of his hands and body on her. Who knew that being so totally bare could be so fucking erotic?

Ian slipped a second finger into her drenched depths and squeezed her buttocks as she writhed on the bed beneath him. Then she wrapped her legs around his hips, and he slid fully over her and settled between her legs. She stroked her hand up and down his erection, spreading the bead of pre-cum with her thumb as she swiped over the tip of his cock. He nudged at her folds each time he rolled his hips forward.

As soon as he rubbed his thumb over her clit she screamed and bit into his shoulder, and her hips bucked upward. Every muscle in her body tightened, and then let go into liquid heat as her orgasm rolled through her, and left her shaking in his arms, gasping. Ian held her until her breathing regulated and she stilled beneath him. With a deep kiss, he eased his fingers out of her and rolled to lay on his side next to her limp body.

She wanted to take care of him, she really did, but already exhaustion laid lead weights on her eyelids. Ian kissed her cheeks, her nose, her eyes, and back to her lips. 'Get some rest. We've got all night.'

'I love you so much, Ian.'

He sucked in a breath, kissed her some more, then said words she'd wanted to hear from him for a long time, 'I love you more than life, Denise.'

With the last of her energy, she pulled him in for a tongue tingling kiss, and then sleep claimed her.

When she next roused, Ian lay snoozing by her side, with one leg draped over hers. Goosebumps rippled up her arms and down her spine and she shivered. Ian stirred, took one look at her, and cursed. 'Let's get you covered up. I'm sorry, honey.'

She ran her thumb over his tight lips. 'Don't be. It was fun.' She grinned. 'Besides, I'm sure you have ways of warming me up again.'

He kissed the tip of her thumb, which sent tingles through her belly, and then lifted off the bed. A disappointed mewl came from her when he tugged his jeans up and raised the zipper. Ian shot her a smile and raised his eyebrows. 'I'm not planning on keeping these on for long. Just until I get you into bed.'

His words had her immediately wet between the legs and heat pooled low. 'Get this dress off me, right now, mister.'

His low chuckle and the gleam in his eyes had her desperate for his touch. Ian undressed her at a slow, tantalising pace with gentle hands. By the time he pulled the duvet up over her naked body, she was ready to explode. He stood beside the bed and undressed himself at the same maddening speed, and when he finally climbed onto the mattress, she grabbed hold of his bobbing erection and pulled him to her eager mouth.

Startled, he twitched and nearly overbalanced, and had to grab the headboard to hold himself up. Denise sucked him in and out of her mouth, and licked her tongue around his broad tip. He tasted salty and creamy, and a vein bulged down one side of his engorged cock. Denise ran light fingers along it, and he twitched inside her mouth. Pleasuring him raised Denise's excitement, and she needed release soon. She eased a hand between her legs and rubbed her swollen clit while Ian straddled her chest and ground his hips into her face.

'Oh God, baby, I'm not gonna last long if you keep going.'

She felt torn. Oh so badly, she wanted him to come in her mouth, but she also needed him inside her. She wanted to do everything at once with him. It didn't feel like anywhere near enough to concentrate on only one thing at a time. She moaned around his cock, and he yelled, 'Oh fuck,' and bucked against her, gripping the headboard. He spilled into her mouth, over her lips, and down her chin while his cock pulsed and he rode her face. She pinched her clit and cried out as a small orgasm took her.

Ian slipped from between her lips and knelt there, panting and holding the headboard like it would stop him from drowning. 'Oh shit, woman.'

Denise giggled, and then wiped her hand across her lips and

chin. Ian cursed again and eased to his feet, then went to the sink and brought back a wet washcloth, which he used to wipe her clean. All done, he disappeared again, and Denise heard the tap running while he rinsed the cloth.

Seconds later, he came to bed and climbed beneath the duvet with her. 'Your turn,' he whispered, and his breath tickled her ear.

Ian ducked under the quilt and slid his body down the bed until he came to rest between her spread legs. He slid his fingers up and down her wet channel a couple of times, and then he shoved his face between her thighs. She'd never had a man's tongue inside her before, and—Oh God—it felt bloody wonderful. He circled it around her clit, and then plunged into her.

With tongue and fingers, he pleasured her, and she climaxed fast and hard. Ian lapped up her juices and kept up his caresses, dragging her from one orgasm to the next, until she couldn't cope with any more sensation and had to beg him to stop. With a low, satisfied chuckle, he kissed first one inner thigh, then the other, and then lifted himself back up the bed. On his side, he pulled Denise into him and wrapped her in his arms, where they fell asleep together.

They didn't wake until Maureen arrived in the morning. Instead of going home for the day, as he usually did, Ian unpacked his holdall and settled in with Denise, helping the nurse whenever he could. Whether Denise wanted to talk, or needed to sleep—whatever—he stayed by her side. There for her.

The day passed in broken stages. One moment Denise would be in the middle of saying something, and the next, she'd be waking up with the sunlight coming from a new direction, and Ian much further through the book he read whenever she slept. Only once had she awoken to find the armchair vacant and Ian nowhere in sight. He hadn't stayed away long, and came back in smelling (and tasting) of coffee and cake.

Although Denise managed sips of water, and a quarter cup of coffee, she couldn't bear even the thought of food. Nobody fussed too much over her lack of appetite by then, as it was expected, and the drip gave her what she needed, as well as her pain meds.

The night followed nearly the same pattern, with the main change being Ian snuggling into bed next to her and cuddling her while they slept. Then whispering sweet nothings to her when she woke. They kissed and stroked one another, but no more. Denise had used up her energy reserves the previous day and night, and needed to build them up again. At no point did she pick up on any frustration on his part, only a quiet contentment as he lay with her. Denise's mood felt a strange mix of sad and joyful … poignant yet deeply soothing.

Maureen arrived the next morning with Sally and a crowd of other folks, all bearing gifts. Some brought food, others drink, while her two favourite nurses took care of flowers and prettying Denise up for her wedding in the afternoon. Maureen produced a sleek little cream cotton dress, decorated with lace trim. Its fit was a little on the loose side, but Sally took care of that with discreetly placed pins. Maureen offered her a matching silk headscarf, but Denise shook her head. She'd feel a lot more comfortable without it.

The many hands made light work of moving furniture around to make room for the ceremony and celebration. While tradition would have dictated that Ian not see her on the eve of their wedding, her situation offered a certain level of dispensation, and they only banished him when it came time to dress her up.

Father Andrews was a small, slight man with a big personality. Denise took an instant liking to him, and it pleased her that he would be the one to marry them. They kept the ceremony brief but sweet. When Ian produced a thin gold band and slipped it onto her ring finger, a thrill of pleasant surprise brought tears to her eyes. A ring was the last thing she'd expected in all the hurry.

Maureen's husband took a few photos for Ian, and then it was done. Denise slept through most of the after party, which they kept short. The house emptied on the wings of well wishes and tears. How could it be that such relative strangers could give her so much more love than her family had done in her final months?

In the early evening, Ian called it a night and got her undressed and into bed. He took care to pack the dress back into its protective plastic sleeve and hung it up. Through sleepy lids, Denise asked him to leave her nightie in its drawer. Even if they didn't manage anything, she wanted to lay skin to skin with him. Naked, standing by the edge of the bed, Ian said, 'Move over, Mrs Willis—your man's coming to bed.' Accompanied by her soft laughter, he eased beneath the duvet and pulled her close.

The early part of the night followed much the same pattern as the night prior, but a little after one o'clock, Denise came into her second wind. Joyfully, she spread her sails and rode the breeze.

Her kisses brought Ian to full wakefulness, and her hand had him standing to attention in no time at all. He kissed her and let his hands roam, and soon had her whimpering and writhing with need. When he lay atop her, nudging at her wet and throbbing entrance, the anticipation felt almost unbearable. But that was nothing compared to when he pushed into her and lay fully sheathed within.

Although not particularly big, he knew how to use it, and hit all the right places. And his hands, lips, and tongue took care of the rest. Oh, to have him inside her at last. He kept the pace slow yet firm, making sure she benefitted from every inch of him.

This stage in the game absolved them from having to worry about silly things like contraception, and riding him bareback felt so utterly awesome. It took a long time for them to climax, and when they did the universe imploded around them, wrapping them in a tiny bubble of bliss, where nothing else existed but the two of them. Their bodies pressed tight together and limbs entangled. Panting and crying out in unison.

Denise's orgasm rocked her heart, mind, body, and soul. It built deliciously slowly, and rolled through at the same devastating rate, until it left her sobbing in Ian's arms. He kissed her tears away and held her close through the night. Denise drifted to sleep untroubled in the knowledge that she could die happy now.

True to his promise, Ian stayed with her until the end. When she moved into Saint Catherine's Hospice, he moved right in with her, and never left her side. They shared so much together, and Denise felt that she got to live another thirty-five years in those last eight hundred and forty hours.

The best part of each of those thirty-five days was waking up next to him. And the best part of those nights, going to sleep in the knowledge he would be there to ease her back into the world in the morning, and to banish the terrors of the dark that crept up from time to time.

No matter how bad things got, how scary it might be, all she had to do was curl up in his arms, and it would all be okay again. More than okay. Good times had never felt so good.

In the quiet hours of Thursday morning, Denise fell into a sleep from which she wouldn't awake. Soft birdsong accompanied her final thoughts—the memory of the spark and fire of falling in love with Ian, her soulmate. Safe and comforted within his warm embrace, sharing their breath and love as she said goodbye to a life fully lived, she slipped away quietly, sinking gently beneath still waters, and rested easy in joy and gratitude for such an end to the best of days.

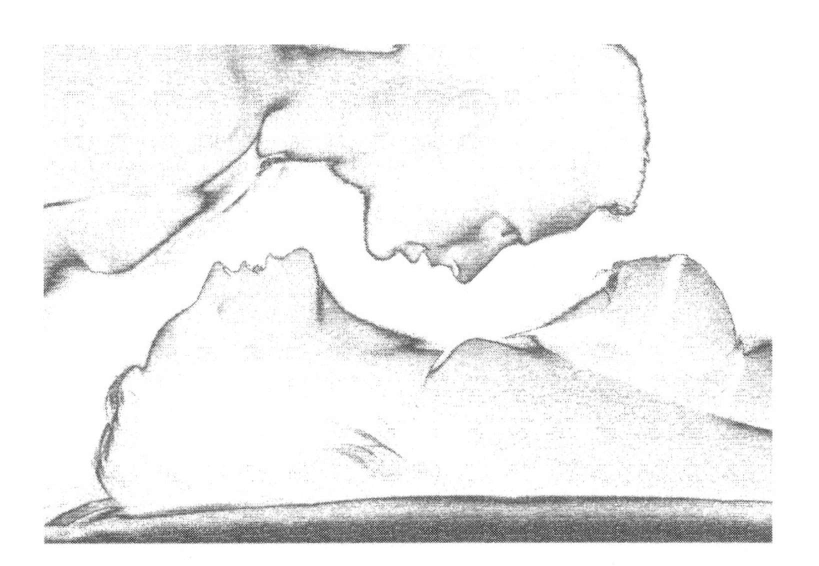

CHAPTER EIGHT

Overboard

The Elloise set out from Coffs Harbour just outside Brisbane, bathed in sunshine and anticipation. This promised to be an easy gig—waitressing the luxury yacht on a scenic sail across the Pacific to Monterey Bay.

Nine days out, enthusiastically engaged in island hopping, Stella's boss made it clear that she'd underestimated what *duties* he expected of her. Unfortunately, he chose his moment while lounging on the aft deck at sunset, bourbon in hand.

Resistant to his advances, a struggle ensued, and when Stella fell overboard, the bastard didn't stop; just threw a life jacket after her. And, while the waters were warm, they held more than Stella and the fast receding Elloise. Sharks could quite well be keeping her company even now. Abruptly, Stella stopped yelling and thrashing around, and instead, did her best to relax and just float with the current.

Daylight came. And went. Came again—with nothing more in sight than more ocean, and more importantly, no shark fins —yet. Dehydrated and suffering sunstroke, Stella soon lost track. The punishing rays beat down relentlessly, and the freely available water mocked her parched lips. The gentle rocking of the calm sea gave false promise of protection—Stella wanted to know what hand rocked this particular cradle, God or the Devil?

Sometime during a black and moonless night, she hit land. Or did it hit her? Did it matter? Rocks and surf pummelled her to shore, where she collapsed to the abrasive sand, half-drowned. And still the waves pretended to caress. Stella passed out, praying that a local would soon find her. Silly girl, she ought to have remembered to be careful what she asked for.

For sure, a native dragged her out of the surf, but he wasn't quite what she'd had in mind. Big hands and muscled arms lifted her from the sodden beach and carried her off into the trees. After being jostled up and down for a long time, her rescuer laid her on what felt like some kind of woven matting. In the pitch blackness, something rough and hard pressed to her lips while those strong arms held her in a seated position. Stella flinched, still mostly delirious from sunstroke, dehydration, and exhaustion.

The unknown and so-far-non-communicative helper persisted until she opened her lips. Water had never tasted so good. Pure, fresh, delicious, life-giving water. Thirsty as she was, he only let her take a little before pulling the vessel away. Within moments of him easing her back down onto the matting, Stella fell asleep. Only to awake shivering with teeth chattering. Rustling came out of the darkness, and then her saviour eased down next to her and pulled her into him, so that they lay spooned. He wrapped his arms and legs around her, and his heat and comfort lulled her into a deep slumber.

Bright sunlight roused her, although Stella rather wished it hadn't. The glare hurt her head. In fact, everything seemed to hurt everywhere. Stiff and sore and thirsty, Stella sat up and blinked, then surveyed her surroundings. Woven palm fronds protected her from the sun, and a refreshing breeze reached her as it blew through the canopy. Beneath her, lay more of the woven frond stuff, which lay atop a mix of foliage, sand, and rocks. Movement on the edge of the little clearing snagged her attention and halted her roaming eyes.

A tall, muscled, dark figure emerged from the trees. Aside from a tattered pair of canvas shorts that barely covered the essentials, he wore nothing. The sun glistened on his sweat-soaked, honey-brown torso. And what a glorious sight that was. Ripped abs. Bulging pecs and arms … bulging everything. Those shorts seemed far too small for the enormous man standing before her. Stella couldn't help but sit and stare, mouth agape.

Then he stepped forward, running a hand through his short black hair, and gave her a smile.

'Hello?' she tried.

'Aloha.' His voice sounded surprisingly soft and melodic for such a big guy.

Stella recognised the Hawaiian greeting, and her heart both rose and sank at the same time. Rose because she'd obviously ended up on an island close enough to civilisation for the natives to speak a language she knew of. Sank because Stella had no clue how to speak it or understand it, other than that one word.

'Do you speak English?'

His smile faltered. '`A`ole maopopo ia`u.'

Dismayed, Stella told him, 'I have no clue what you just said.'

The man took another step forward and settled into a crouch at the edge of the clearing.

Stella tried a different tack, 'I'm Stella.' She pointed at her chest.

His smile blossomed again, and he nodded and said, 'Kaimi.'

'Nice to meet you.' Stella smiled, hoping he at least got the gist of her meaning.

'Pôloli?'

Stella could only sit and squint at him. He shook his head, and then made a beak with his fingers and thumb and raised it to his mouth a couple of times. Then realisation dawned—Kaimi mimed eating. Stella nodded. 'Yes. Hungry.'

This time, he smiled big enough to show teeth. Nice, white, straight pearls that told her he must have had access to a dentist in his recent past. Another good sign, but if she couldn't communicate with him, how could she ever get him to understand that she needed to get off the island? An idea struck her, and she mimed swimming.

Kaimi's smile fell off a cliff, and he shook his head over and over again. 'A'ole. A'ole.' Then he did a brilliant impression of a shark fin gliding through water. No wonder he looked so upset; he thought she wanted to go for a swim. The sound that escaped her lips couldn't make up its mind whether it was a laugh, a snort, or a sob.

More disheartened by the second, Stella said, 'Boat?' while also trying to mimic rowing. The good news was that he understood her. The bad, that he shook his head some more. So, no boat. Okay then. When she didn't speak again, Kaimi repeated his 'Pôloli?' and eating mime. Not having any better ideas, Stella nodded. Kaimi leapt to his feet and rushed to a metal box nestled at the back of the shelter.

When he lifted the lid, Stella looked on, deeply curious. Kaimi lifted out a couple of tins and a heavy-looking sack. Well, it seemed she'd avoided the fate of having to eat something gross like raw fish or bugs. Perhaps she did have an angel or two on her side after all. He held a tin out to her and showed her the label. Stella couldn't read the writing, but did recognise the picture of curry. From the sack, Kaimi scooped a handful of rice to show her. Relieved, Stella nodded and smiled. 'Yes, please.'

While Kaimi got busy cooking, which involved fetching water to heat from a bucket at the back of their shelter and building a cook fire, Stella thought about her situation. How long had she been missing? No sure answer presented itself, though; too many lost hours at sea. Not that it made a difference—nobody she knew would expect her to resurface for a couple of months. Stella had told everyone about her planned yacht stint and that she'd likely not be able to email or text for much of the time. Talking of texting …

'Kaimi?'

He turned around.

'Phone?' Stella stuck out her thumb and little finger to mime a phone to her ear.

Kaimi shook his head. Damn it. Resigned, she smiled and signalled for him to continue with his cooking.

Well, her native wore modern-seeming shorts, had actual tinned food with him, and spoke Hawaiian, so he couldn't be that isolated, could he? That calmed her a little. All she had to work around was the communication thing. Then the enormity of that loomed large, and her shoulders slumped. Then a fat tear rolled down her cheeks, and another soon followed.

'Oh sod it.' Stella fell into full on weeping. Not normally given over to emotion or dramatics, the outburst took her by surprise. Not as much as it did Kaimi, though. He dropped the wooden spoon into the cook pot and spun around, wide-eyed. Unfortunately, she didn't seem able to stop.

Two strides brought him to her side, and he dropped to his knees and wrapped his arms around her, pulling her head to his chest. Through his well-rounded muscles, Stella heard his heart doing a rapid thump-thump. His warmth and strength enveloped her, and she snuggled in, calming quickly but not wanting to let go just yet.

Out at sea, Stella had felt convinced that she would die a horrible death, alone. The physical contact, while comforting, also brought all the loneliness and fear back to her. Once her sobs subsided, Kaimi eased her away and looked down at her tear-streaked face. With a crooked finger, he wiped her cheeks dry. What he did next, had her sucking in a breath. He raised the finger to his full lips and tasted her upset, looking into her eyes all the while. Stella's brain stuttered, and her stomach fluttered. The gesture struck her as both sweet and incredibly erotic. Even while some of the ice inside her melted, something else hardened. Something wearing canvas shorts.

Crushed against his body as she was, Stella couldn't exactly avoid it. Her cheeks heated. Had he seen the flare of desire in her eyes? What signals had she just given? When he bent his lips to her mouth, her vulnerability struck her full force. No matter how loudly she might scream, she doubted anybody would be within hearing distance. But that was just silly of her —he could have taken her last night if he'd wanted to, and a lot more easily than now. Then Kaimi let her go, turned a stiff back on her, and strode back to the fire. He'd felt her tense up, and now she worried she'd upset him. The man had been nothing but kind.

They didn't communicate or look at one another again until the rice and curry had cooked, and Kaimi brought a steaming bowlful to her. His approach screamed of hesitance and caution, and Stella felt that she ought to try and smooth things over. With a big smile, she accepted the meal and said, 'Thank you.'

His frown lifted a little, and a tiny bit of light entered his eyes as he nodded. After serving himself, Kaimi dropped down to the matting, taking care to sit right at the edge to give her plenty of space. Stella swallowed her useless pride along with the mouthful of rice, and said, 'I'm sorry, Kaimi.' With a shrug, she added, 'It's me. Not you.'

Even if he couldn't understand her words, he might catch her drift. His rich brown eyes held her gaze for a moment, and then he nodded at her raised spoon. 'Maika`i?'

Stella smiled and said, 'Yes, it's good, thank you.'

Silence cloaked them again, but of a lighter weave than before. When they'd finished eating, Kaimi fetched water. Stella recognised the rough feel from the previous night. Hand carved wooden cups. Was this how he passed his time? And what was he doing out here in the first place? Then an awful thought occurred to her. Had he been stranded here too? Was she seeing the last of dwindling supplies? Surely not. The chances of two people washing up on the same island. No. No way. Uh uh. Stop thinking like that.

To distract herself, and attempt to make things up to Kaimi, Stella helped him do the clean up. Afterward, he handed her a pole with a bucket dangling at either end. Then, machete in hand, he led them into the jungle. The deeper they went, the higher the humidity climbed, and soon Stella found herself sopping wet through. Her skimpy waitress blouse turned see through and clingy, while the short tight skirt proved totally useless. Not only did it fail to protect her legs at all, but it hindered her from navigating the tangled undergrowth and fallen tree limbs. Eventually, fed up with the stupid thing, Stella ripped it up its side seams so she could stride instead of taking baby-steps. And when the next obstacle arrived, she threw her leg over it with no problem. Modesty was overrated anyhow. And, she kind of liked the appraising looks that Kaimi shot her way periodically. When Stella stumbled, her cute native caught her in his arms and held her close, preventing her from falling. With a grin, he planted a quick kiss on her lips and then let her go. Flushed and flustered, Stella retrieved the buckets and pole and followed behind. He had a nice, tight set of glutes. The way his buttocks bunched and flexed with each step had her wanting to give them a squeeze.

By the time they reached the waterfall and lagoon, sweat soaked her from head to toe, and her hair lay slicked against her scalp. Thirst burned her throat, and she had to stand bent at the waist and panting for a few minutes to recover. As soon as they stopped, Kaimi took the pole and buckets from her and sauntered over to the water as if they'd just taken a gentle Sunday stroll. Any annoyance fled, though, when he gestured her over and showed her how to drink by scooping a curved, waxy leaf into the water. All she wanted to do was dive into the deep pool, but that might contaminate their drinking supply. Best to follow his lead.

Kaimi squatted at the pool edge and filled each bucket in turn, then hooked them back onto the pole. Rather than pick it up, he stood and shucked out of his shorts. Even though he turned his back to her, Stella still got an eyeful of arse. It looked good enough to eat, like a nice ripe plum. And then, when he twisted around to gesture her forward, she got a look at his tackle too. Oh, wow. Soft though he may be, he was huge. Not so long, by the look of it, but thick.

Stella dragged her eyes away from his package and was relieved when he just turned back to the pool—hopefully without noticing her distraction. At the splash of Kaimi diving in, Stella forgot about any concerns and jumped right in after him, not bothering to undress. Her blouse and skirt could do with a wash. Oh, the cool dip felt delicious. Just the refreshment she'd needed. While she treaded water, Kaimi swam toward the waterfall, and once there, lifted himself out onto a flat rock just in front of the spray. Stella swam to join him, and when she got there, he grabbed her at her under arms to help her heave herself out.

Accidentally, his large hands brushed the sides of her breasts, and a flash of excitement rippled through her body. Her nipples had already turned to stone from the chill of the water. They locked eyes, and Kaimi froze, forgetting to let go of her. Stella knelt by him, chest heaving, as desire swamped her. Her tongue flicked out, and she licked her lips. Kaimi's eyes widened. Then Stella eased forward and brushed her mouth over his. He sat still for a moment, and then pulled her in with his hand at the back of her head. His lips mashed against hers, and then his tongue nudged at her seam, and she parted for him.

While his tongue wrapped around hers, his hands rubbed up and down her back. Passion swallowed all coherent thought, and Stella hooked a leg sideways and wriggled until she knelt astride his lap. If his toned body and smell hadn't been enough to set her on fire, his taste was. As she settled down on top of him, he cupped her buttocks in his hands and squeezed. Between her legs, his erection grew, and Stella regretted not stripping down before getting in the pool. Still, her flimsy panties weren't much of a barrier.

She moaned and rubbed against his groin, while he reached between them and fondled her breasts. Then he trailed kisses along her jaw, down her neck, over her collarbone, and eventually sucked a breast into his mouth, where he nibbled at her through the thin fabric. Fire shot from nipple to core, and she arched her spine to feed him more.

With shaking hands, Stella unfastened her buttons and pushed her blouse off her shoulders. Kaimi took over and shoved the garment the rest of the way off. Then he worked her bra clasp open and divested her of that too. His tongue latched onto her bared nipples while he reached between her legs and pushed her lace panties aside. He slid his finger between her wet folds and thrust into her slick entrance. His rock-hard cock rubbed at her as she writhed above him and held the back of his head.

Stella mewled in ecstasy when Kaimi eased another finger inside her and circled her clit with his thumb. Raw need ached deep within and she got so drenched that her juices coated her thighs, and his fingers made wet noises as he slid them in and out of her pussy. Then he found her mouth again and plunged his tongue into her while flipping her onto her back, fingers still planted deep.

Knelt between her legs, he watched her as he fucked her with his hand. Then he nudged her knees to her shoulders, so that she lay there fully exposed. A needy whimper broke from her when he pulled his fingers out of her and left her empty. With a soft smile, Kaimi took hold of her panties and, in a single yank, ripped them off her. Oh fuck, that was hot.

Satisfied, he pushed her knees back to her shoulders and planted his head between her thighs. He circled her clit with his tongue, and then sucked it into his mouth. Stella screamed beneath him and rocked her hips. As mind-blowing as this felt, she needed filling. Soon. In tune with her needs, he plunged fingers into her and fucked her while continuing to eat her clit. Her walls stretched, on the edge of tolerance, and Stella realised he'd sunk everything but his thumb into her, all the way down to the V between thumb and fingers.

Kaimi stroked her between pussy and buttocks, dragging her juices along for the ride, and when he had her good and coated, he pushed his thumb into her back entrance. Fireworks exploded behind Stella's eyes and a high, keening wail forced its way up her throat to freedom. She bucked beneath him in an erratic rhythm and clenched around him. Orgasm after orgasm tore through her, and Kaimi didn't stop—kept going and took her through one into another and another, until she stilled beneath him, spent and gasping.

While Stella lay on her back recovering, Kaimi leaned sideways and dipped his head beneath the waterfall. Seconds later, he returned to her side and kissed her thoroughly, a happy smile on his face. 'Maika`i?' he asked.

Stella chuckled and said, 'Mmm, yes. Very Maika`i.'

With another lingering kiss, he eased her to her feet and steered her beneath the deliciously cool spray, where he proceeded to massage the water through her hair, squeezing out every last drop of the seawater she'd almost drowned in. That done, he moved down her torso, running his hands down the deep valley between her breasts. Then he pulled her skirt down and dropped it on the rocks next to her blouse. His hand slid all the way back up her legs until it reached her pussy, and he fondled her some more.

Then he turned her around so that her back rested against his ripped abs, and brought his hands to her breasts. His erection nudged against her buttocks, and Stella moved her feet to each side to open up for him. Kaimi paused to bite her shoulder, and then he bent her forward at the waist and braced her hands against the rock face of the cliff. Positioned at her wet and engorged lips, he ran his hands down her spine and rubbed at the cleft between her buttocks. Then he thrust into her while his hands grabbed hold of her hips and pulled her into his groin.

He took her hard and fast, and Stella would have stumbled forward if not for the firm grip he had on her. His thick shaft stretched her to her max, and she felt every inch of him while he moved in and out. Each thrust gave him full penetration, and her walls locked around his cock as her climax built. Her knees buckled when she came, and his strong arms took her weight.

Kaimi pounded into her from behind, and while she cried out in the throes of ecstasy, he thrust harder and faster until his hips locked up and he bit down on her shoulder with a muffled grunt. His cock pulsed inside her and shot hot cum, sending another wave of orgasm through her.

They stood tangled together for a while, getting their breath back. Then Kaimi pulled out and guided Stella back into the full force of the spray. There, he washed her down, and then took care of himself. Unabashed, she watched. When he let go of himself, Stella reached out and stroked him. With a grin, he pulled her in for a kiss, then swatted her on the backside before pushing her back toward the rock shelf where her clothes lay.

Stella bent and retrieved her stuff. Her panties were long past their best, and beyond wearing, so she slipped into her skirt and blouse, and decided to bury her underwear back at the beach. It seemed pointless and a little absurd to wear a bra without panties, and she'd never found bras that comfy anyhow. Instead of fastening her blouse all the way down, Stella tied the bottom half just below her breasts, leaving her abdomen exposed. It felt so much more comfortable that way.

Silent, they swam back through the pool to the far bank. Kaimi pulled on his shorts and picked up the machete, which he handed to Stella, then he stooped and shouldered the pole and water buckets. Weak and wobbly from her numerous orgasms, Stella felt grateful that he'd taken the heavy job. Before she turned to head back through the jungle, she rose on tip toes and gave him a soft, sensuous kiss.

All the way back to camp, Stella pondered over what they'd just shared. How come she'd repelled her boss's advances so arduously, only to throw herself at Kaimi? They were two completely different men, for one. Her native was kind and considerate, and communicated far better despite the hindrance of not sharing a language. Whereas her boss had been the exact opposite of all of those. Kaimi seemed to appreciate her body and what she'd just given him, whereas the rich bastard who'd left her to drown or get eaten by sharks, didn't just take it for granted, but assumed he had some God-given right to her. The prick.

Back at the beach, Kaimi secured the water at the back of the canopy and put heavy lids on top of them. Stella admired the set up he had, and wondered again how come he was here. Once they'd gotten sorted out, Stella went for a nap, still recovering from her ordeal at sea.

When Kaimi awakened her, shouting and gesticulating wildly, the sky had grown black and threatening. Stella blinked herself awake and sat up. The air felt leaden—almost too heavy to suck in a breath. The horizon had a yellow tint to it, and whitecaps broke up the blue of the ocean. The two of them got busy tying down everything they could, and Kaimi showed Stella with gestures and mimes what he needed her to do.

Once they had everything as secure as they could make it,

Kaimi took Stella by the hand and pulled her into the trees. Perturbed, she followed him deep into the jungle. By the time he eased them to a stop, her arm ached from the drag he'd put on it in his haste. The wind whipped through the upper canopy, and even this far inland, she could hear the waves as they crashed thunderously ashore. Would the camp survive the storm?

In front of her, Kaimi ducked down and parted low hanging branches to reveal a shallow rock overhang. He bent down and brushed the soft sand at its floor, then motioned for Stella to join him. She dropped to hands and knees and crawled in after him. Kaimi lay on his side, back pressed against the solid rear wall, and indicated that she should squeeze down next to him. Stella wriggled around until she lay spooned against him. With the branches back in place at the entrance, the small space felt quite cosy, and the wind didn't penetrate. Nor did the rain, when it came, even as torrential as it was. The temperature dropped alarmingly, and kept on dropping as darkness ate the day.

For the second night in a row, Kaimi wrapped his arms and legs around Stella and held her close. Neither one of them got much sleep with the storm raging. Stella offered up a prayer of thanks that this hadn't hit while she'd been adrift. For sure, she would have died. When Stella trembled and whimpered at an extra-loud crash of thunder, Kaimi stroked her abdomen with his thumb and nuzzled her neck, all the while making calming noises. All about them, the wind roared, and trees cracked and snapped.

Timid, the daylight crept in on slow feet and with half a heart. Even when Kaimi led them out of the trees and back onto the beach, the sun remained dim, obscured behind a wall of clouds. A cry escaped when Stella saw the devastation. Kaimi's camp had been obliterated. Had they stayed there during the night, they would have been seriously injured from the flying debris. Not to mention the high waves that looked to have reached much farther inland than usual, judging by the new high-tide line. Stella wondered how the Elloise had fared.

Had its idiot owner found safe harbour? A large part of her hoped not, while a teeny tiny bit felt guilty for wishing him ill.

Kaimi took a moment to pull her into a warm, solid embrace, and ask her, 'Maika`i?'

Stella nodded. He probably wasn't saying 'good' this time, but most likely something similar, like asking if she was okay. Either way, she got the gist and wanted to reassure him. Satisfied, he eased away and surveyed the wreckage of what had been his home. Then he got busy. Together, they cleared the space as best they could and took stock of what could be salvaged and what couldn't. A new roof and walls would have to be made, and the bed and bedding had been taken, either by wind or wave. The heavy metal box had saved their food supplies, as had the lids on top of the water buckets. A slim palm-type tree had fallen atop the buckets and thus anchored them in place. A lot of scratches, curses, and sweating later, they rolled the limb a foot away, and used it as a base upon which to build a rudimentary shelter.

For the rest of the day, shortened by cloud cover, they worked like demons, and by nightfall had somewhere safe and dry to sleep. In the middle of the afternoon, Kaimi had disappeared into the trees in search of dry kindling, which—despite Stella's doubts—he managed to find. Perhaps he knew of more rocky shelter that may have kept the worst of the weather off the wood. As early dusk descended, Kaimi got a fire going, and Stella helped to put together a meal of rice and canned beans and vegetables. They'd lost their bowls and utensils in the storm, but fortunately, the pans had been with the food. Kaimi showed Stella how to fashion plates out of large, waxy leaves, and they ate with fingers.

Afterward, Kaimi banked the fire. They curled up next to it with a bottle of dark spirit that burned going down and made Stella cough at the first couple of sips. The bottle didn't have a label—home brew, maybe? They passed the bottle back and forth, and Stella missed being able to banter. It would have been romantic with the firelight and the alcohol, especially now the breeze had dropped. Kaimi's constant touching made a good substitute for talk, though, and Stella reciprocated as they snuggled.

Gradually, his attentions turned more passionate, and his arousal nudged at her buttocks. Stella wriggled against him and pressed her bottom into his groin. Kaimi kissed her neck and worked a hand inside her blouse, where he rubbed her nipples. His other hand snaked beneath the hem of her skirt and slid between her thighs. Stella reached behind and between them and tugged down his zipper, then reached into his shorts and pulled him free. He lay thick and hard in her palm, and groaned in her ear when she worked up and down his shaft.

A bead of thick, creamy moisture slicked her thumb as she stroked the head of his cock. He nudged her legs apart with a knee, and Stella hooked her upper leg over his hip. Kaimi circled her clit, and then pushed a finger inside her. Within a few seconds, she grew wet and turned on as hell. He kissed up her neck, along her jaw, and then settled on her lips and plundered her mouth with his tongue. The kiss deepened, and he worked two more fingers into her slick entrance, then moved them in and out while rubbing her clit with his thumb. Stella moaned into his mouth, and he bit her bottom lip then sucked on it. He tugged at the knot of her blouse with his free hand, and Stella untied it and eased it open, then went back to his erection.

A mewl of protest broke free when he abandoned her to shuck out of his shorts, and Kaimi chuckled. Then he rolled her onto her stomach and pushed her knees beneath her hips, so her ass raised in the air, exposing her pussy. Kaimi parted her wet folds and lowered his head so he could lick and suck at her clit. Stella's hips bucked, and she gave a loud cry of pleasure. She needed him inside her, and her walls clenched in want while she writhed at his ministrations, but he refused to give her what she desired. Instead, he flicked his tongue around her entrance and teased her clit. 'Kami, please,' she whispered.

For answer, he kissed his way up her spine, and stroked her with his fingers. He couldn't understand her words, and still she begged, 'Kaimi, fuck me, please. I need you.' His groan showed her that he'd gotten the message. The tease still refused her, though, and bit her shoulder before moving to her neck where he sucked and nipped. His erection rubbed between her buttocks while his fingers rubbed and pinched her clit. Just when she felt as though she couldn't take any more, Kaimi flipped her onto her back and covered her. Knelt between her legs, he positioned himself at her entrance and pushed into her.

It took three gentle thrusts to see him planted in her up to the base of his cock, and his balls rubbed at her buttocks. Stella wrapped her legs around his waist and pulled him in for a lingering kiss. As he plundered her with his tongue, he penetrated her with his cock. Even as wet as she was, he was so thick that she felt every millimetre of him, and her walls tightened at the delicious friction.

Where the sex had been fast and rough yesterday, tonight it came slow and sensuous. Kaimi rocked in and out of her, and his firm pecks rubbed at her nipples, sending lightning from her breasts to her core. 'Oh, Kaimi,' Stella murmured. She tried to increase the tempo beneath him, but he—maddeningly—kept it slow and steady. The frustration drove her wild. Her periodic pleas descended into one long moan of frustrated pleasure, and her nerves tingled and zinged. And still her orgasm built. She couldn't possibly take much more. Each thrust brought exquisite torture, and Stella raked her nails down Kaimi's back while they rocked together.

Only when she'd grown wild with need did he pick up the pace and plunge into her harder and faster. When the orgasm broke over her in waves, Stella screamed and bucked beneath him. She buried her head in his shoulder, and he pumped her hard—firm enough to drive her over the bed of fronds they'd laid down earlier. Then he stiffened in her arms and grunted into her neck. His cock pulsed inside her, and heat filled her as he spilled his seed.

Spent, they lay in one another's arms, panting, and slicked with sweat. They fell asleep with Kaimi's thick length still inside her.

The morning brought bright sun and clear skies, and more love making.

And a boat.

Stella squinted into the distance to try and get a better look, even while her heart raced. A half-hour later, it grew from a smudge on the horizon to a recognisable small craft. Beside her, Kaimi waved and grinned. 'Akamu,' he kept telling her, but Stella had no idea what that word meant. Was it someone's name? What the little boat was called? Whatever, Kaimi seemed to be pleased to see it. As, of course, was Stella. Although, she also felt a twinge of concern. What would the arrival of company mean to Kaimi and her?

Nervous, she fussed and fidgeted with her attire, which now felt seriously inadequate. Kaimi picked up on her ambivalence, and tried to reassure her with touch and attention. By the time the boat anchored out at sea, Stella was about ready to climb trees. While she watched the small motorboat chug toward shore, she had to remind herself to breathe.

A lone man piloted the boat, which drew to a stop a few yards out from the gently sloping beach. Then he jumped into the surf and dragged the small metal craft onto the sand. He stood a few inches shorter than Kaimi, but otherwise they could have passed for twins. Perhaps they were. Kaimi jogged to him and gave him a hug. Then he turned to Stella, wearing a delighted grin, and said, 'Akamu.'

Stella nodded and offered a tight smile. The newcomer studied her, curiosity etched into every line of his face. While the two men walked across the sand toward her, they babbled together at a fair clip. Akamu seemed to be asking lots of questions. They continued to talk while they headed for the camp, and Stella trailed behind. The men plonked down to the fronds that had replaced the woven matting, and Stella knelt at the edge, feeling out of place.

Then Akamu caught her attention. 'Stella?'

Throat tight, all she could manage was a tiny nod.

'I am Akamu.'

'You speak English?'

He bobbed his head and smiled. 'A little.'

Stella swallowed, unsure what she wanted to ask first. Akamu held up a hand and forestalled the impending torrent. 'Kaimi say he found you on the beach?'

'Yes. I, um, fell overboard.'

Akamu's eyes widened. 'You come long way?'

Stella nodded again. 'Yes. Well, I think so. I drifted for days.'

The two men fell to babbling again, and Stella gnawed at a hangnail while she waited. Then Akamu looked at her again. 'We will take you to mainland.'

'Kaimi too?'

Akamu gave Kaimi a hard look, and Kaimi nodded as if to reiterate something. The silence stretched until it snapped, and Akamu said, 'Yes. Kaimi and I will take you in the boat. Get you help.'

Stella glanced at Kaimi and asked, 'Why is Kaimi here on the island?'

Akamu translated, and they exchanged more words, then he said to Stella, 'Kaimi is on a retreat. He should stay …'

Ah, that explained why Akamu looked unhappy. She'd broken into Kaimi's retreat. Oh dear. How important was it? 'I'm sorry.'

Akamu shook his head. 'It's not your fault. My brother, he saved you, yes?'

'Yes. He took good care of me.'

'Good. I came because of the storm. To check he was … Maika`i … uh …'

'Yes, to see if he was okay.'

Akamu smiled. Nodded. 'Yes. Oh-kay.'

Stella felt bad about breaking into Kaimi's retreat time. 'Is it better for him to stay?'

Akamu shrugged and indicated the damaged camp. 'Need supplies. Make repairs. So, it's good that he comes with me today.' Then what looked like amusement brightened his eyes. 'My brother like you.'

'Oh.' Stella gulped, and pleasure flushed her cheeks. 'I-I like him as well. I so need to learn Hawaiian.'

Akamu laughed. 'My brother say he need to learn English.'

An hour later saw them setting out to sea in the small fishing craft that Akamu had arrived in, with the motorboat roped and trailing behind. On the way, Akamu told her they were headed for a small island called Napari, from where she could take a bigger boat to Hawaii. Once there, she could go to the embassy to get help in getting home.

A pang of loss clenched her stomach. Stella didn't want to go home anymore. She wanted to stay with Kaimi. Would he want that, though? Or had she been a bit of fun? A way to break up the lonely boredom of a retreat? When Stella's face fell along with silence, the two brothers talked together in their rapid-fire Hawaiian tongue. At one point, their voices and expressions grew animated, and Stella felt sure they were arguing. Eventually, Kaimi crossed his arms and repeated one phrase three times in a row, 'Ha`i ia,' growing more heated with each utterance.

With a scowl, Akamu glanced in Stella's direction. Then he turned to survey the ocean ahead and said in a tight voice, 'Kaimi wants you to stay with him.' Then he raised his hands in the air. 'I'm sorry for this. You have your life. My brother doesn't understand.'

Stella leaned forward and placed a hand on Akamu's elbow. 'It's okay. I'm glad you told me.'

Akamu just grunted.

Stella stood and crossed to the short narrow bench that Kaimi sat on and squeezed in next to him. With a smile, she said, 'I want to stay.'

Kaimi looked to Akamu, who translated. When he gazed back at Stella, delight written all over his face, she reached up and pulled him in for a kiss. Just when they were getting into each other, Akamu cleared his throat. With his eyes faced determinedly out to sea, he said, 'We will get to Napari, and will sort it out then.' He stopped, cursed under his breath, then said, 'You don't even know him. You can't speak to each other. How can you hope to communicate well enough—'

Stella had heard plenty and held up a hand. 'We do well enough, thanks.'

Thankfully, Akamu got the message and shut up for the rest of the trip. His displeasure came from him in waves, and she hoped he wouldn't make things more difficult for them than they already were. The sun had dipped low in the sky by the time the boat eased into a small harbour.

'Akamu?'

He met her eyes.

'Thank you for helping. I can see that you must have left early this morning to come see your brother. You seem to be a good man.'

Although he still didn't speak, just gave her a nod, his posture relaxed, and the hard glint in his eyes softened a little.

Once they'd docked, Akamu led them through a small village of wooden huts, some with thatched roofs and others topped with corrugated iron. At the top of a low hill, about half a mile out from the main settlement, he left her and Kaimi alone at a single-storey brick dwelling—substantial by the village standards. Then he continued up the hill after telling her, 'I will speak with the elders.'

With a smile, Kaimi pulled her into the house. He pushed her up against the closed door and pressed his body into her while he leant down and kissed her. Stella wrapped her arms around his shoulders and kissed him back. When his tongue nudged at the seam of her lips, she opened for him, and they deepened their embrace. Low on her belly, his growing arousal nudged at her, and wetness soon coated her between her legs.

Kaimi grabbed her buttocks and squeezed, pulling her into his hard groin. Stella moaned and gripped the back of his head, rising on tip toes to push into him as much as she could. While he licked and sucked at her with his tongue, he ground his hips into her, and they rocked together, making the door bump in its housing.

Then Kaimi lowered his zipper and pushed his shorts off, and his engorged cock bounced in the air—stuck out from his ripped abs. Stella unfastened her blouse and shoved it down her arms. Kaimi pulled it the rest of the way off, and then clamped his mouth around one of her breasts. While he nuzzled at her, he reached a hand between her legs. At her wetness, he groaned and thrust into her with his fingers, which he scissored inside her to stretch her.

Satisfied that she was ready enough, he gripped her beneath her buttocks and lifted her to his hips, pinning her between him and the door. Stella wrapped her legs around him and held onto his shoulders, head thrown back against the door, baring her neck for him. Kaimi positioned himself and thrust into her, hard and delicious, while biting down on her exposed neck. Stella cried out at the rough pounding. 'More,' she cried, and thrust her hips at him to deepen the penetration.

Kaimi got the message and took her hard and fast, making the door bang and rattle behind them as he pummelled her, lips clamped at the base of her neck, where he sucked the soft and vulnerable spot. Stella arched into him, moaning and writhing, and he penetrated her to the max with every thrust.

He came hard and pounded her relentlessly while his cock pulsed inside her, and Stella clenched around him. When he'd finished, still hard, he continued to slide in and out of her, a little more gently, and reached a hand between them to rub at her clit. Stella cried out, so near. By the time Kaimi came again, her orgasm hit her solidly. Kaimi slid to his knees on the floor, and Stella straddled him, kissing their way down from the orgasm.

They had time to clean up, fix food, and then wash the dishes before Akamu came back. Behind him, came a tiny wrinkled man, who looked to Stella to be at least a hundred. He had kind eyes, and she took an instant liking to him. While the men got themselves settled, Stella tried to pick up on whatever clues she could. Akamu seemed a lot more relaxed than when he'd left them. That had to be a good sign, right?

The three men chatted for what felt like a long time, and the elder gave Kaimi a chance to speak at length. Then Akamu translated for her and Iakopa. The gist of it ran along the lines of them wanting to make sure that Stella wasn't being coerced into anything she didn't really want. Next up, were concerns about the authorities and immigration laws. Iakopa declared that Stella needed rest and care before travelling on to Hawaii; at least a month's recuperation, in fact. Of course, she agreed with that readily enough. After that, Akamu would travel to the mainland to make enquiries about their position. In the meantime, Stella would be kept busy with learning Hawaiian.

Well, that was the plan.

In actuality, Kaimi kept her busy in other ways, which proved a lot more fun. The month passed far too quickly. What didn't pass, that should have done, was Stella's period. Oops didn't do it justice—nowhere near. One of the local women checked her over and confirmed her suspicions.

The pregnancy had an upside, however. The elders had another confab and decided that everything possible would be done to keep Stella with them. Akamu left on the boat journey to the mainland in search of answers. It turned out that being a non-US citizen, Stella would need a work visa, which—thanks to her stint on the Elloise—she had for a year. This meant that her employer could apply for a green card for her. Right, like that was so gonna happen. A fleeting thought passed about blackmailing the dick; after all, she'd nearly drowned because of him. Akamu came back with an alternative. At the news, Stella had to sit down, quick. Strange though it may seem, the idea of having Kaimi's baby sat easier than the thought of getting married. She could only shake her head at herself. Surely the child would be the bigger commitment.

It would mean a family green card, though, and Stella could then apply for full residency if she wanted to. About the only thing she felt sure of just then was the fact that she loved Kaimi, and that she wanted to give her child the best life possible, which didn't mean going back to the UK where work had been scarce and the weather and the living difficult. Well then, she had her answer. The small village community got busy planning a traditional island wedding, and Akamu helped Kaimi and Stella deal with the legal side of things.

Another three months saw them happily married, and Stella's bump growing steadily. As time progressed, Kaimi and she developed inventive ways of having sex that were more comfortable for her when she grew big with baby. Her favourite position, though, remained the one he'd taken her by their first time, beneath the waterfall. On her feet, arms braced against the wall, while he fucked her from behind. No surprises that some of the first words she learned had to do with sex.

Better still, Kaimi learned some of her words. The first time he demanded, 'Fuck me now, my woman,' with his heavily accented and lyrical voice, she almost came on the spot. Since then, they'd gotten into rather a nice routine. He would arrive home from his day's labours and come up behind her, where he'd snake his hands around her and cup her full breasts. Then, nuzzling her neck and earlobes, he'd push his erect cock into her lower back and demand, 'Fuck me now, my woman.' Then he'd lift her skirt until it bunched around her waist. Stella had taken to going commando ready for him coming home.

Kaimi would bring her to her first orgasm with his fingers, then he would give her another one with his tongue. By the time he pushed into her, she'd be soaking wet and whimpering on the edge of coming again. A baby, a new life, and a hot and horny husband—Stella couldn't ask for more.

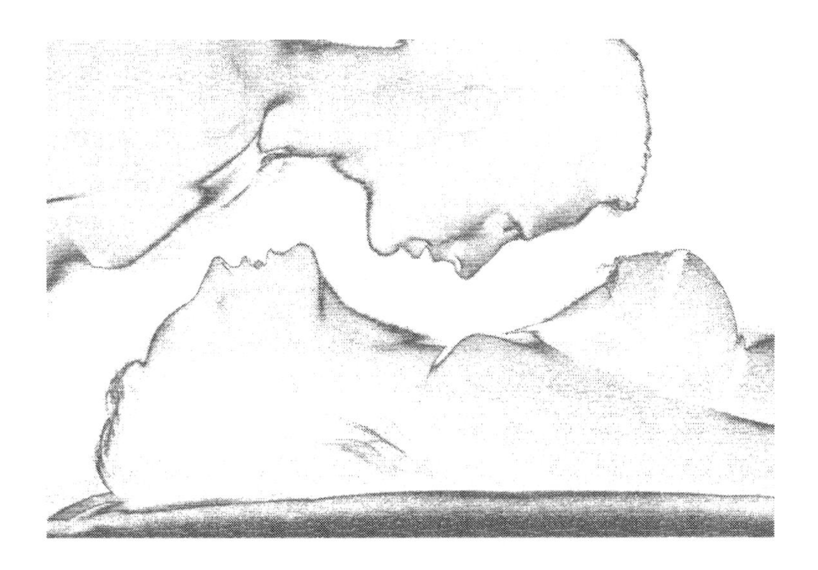

CHAPTER NINE

Alien Liaison

Lunus Two crash-lands on an occupied planet. Things could have been much worse. Even while the dust continues to settle, Marine E8 Ellery takes charge and gets the surviving crew organised. Nine dead, seven injured, and four of us banged up but able bodied. The E8, me (Jay A Hearn—an E6), one of our E4s (McKeehan), and an E2 (Hickory) are all that's left functional out of a crew of twenty.

The E8 calls me over, no doubt to give me yet more duties, but just as I reach his side, a hulking figure approaches the wrecked hull, pausing at the edge of the yawning hole.

I've seen plenty of aliens in my four years of service, but never one as finger licking good as this one. The coalition forces leave Zorth and its inhabitants alone. We have a long history, and most of it not good. Still, at least we've hit somewhere with a breathable atmosphere and an intelligent life form that we can communicate with, even if they hate us more than their nemeses the Zygonian Warlords.

E8 stiffens at my side, then makes a snap decision. 'Hearn, go and see what he wants. A female might be less threatening.'

With a jump to attention, I tell him, 'Yes, Sir.'

Before I can turn away, Ellery orders me to give him my weapon. I suppose I can see his point that the guy has probably come to help, and we don't want to inadvertently start Intergalactic War Five from a silly misunderstanding.

The Zorth watches me with his dark, brooding eyes while I pick my way through the wreckage to him. Closer up, his enormity impresses itself upon me, and as the light strengthens the nearer the open air that I get, it plays over his bulging, rippled muscles. It seems that the Zorths don't bother to cover themselves like we humans do.

Unable to help myself, my gaze drifts to his groin. I mean, nothing wrong with a girl being curious, right? Where a man's cock would be, some kind of ridged sheath bulges out instead. Could he possibly be big enough to fill that pouch? I lick my lips at the thought, then remember where I am and what I'm doing here. Flushed with embarrassment, I drag my gaze back up his awesome, light-grey body. Not a single hair mars his smooth skin. When I meet his eyes, my breath catches in my throat.

Amusement lights his alien features, and he's obviously caught me sneaking a peek. Mortified, and a little nervous at the interest now sharing space with his mirth, I clear my throat and hold out my hand. How do these people greet one another? I have no clue. His dark eyes stare at my hand for a couple of seconds, and then he returns to my face. At length, he grasps my hand and shakes it once.

His grip is at once firm yet gentle, and warm. His skin feels like velvet, and I wonder if the rest of him would be the same. When he's shaken, he keeps hold of my palm, and a low rumble sounds from his chest. Heat pools low in my abdomen, and my heart speeds up. If he ripped my clothes off and took me right here, right now, I wouldn't stop him. And, for sure, I wouldn't be laying back and thinking of Earth.

I so need to get a hold of myself. Being ship-bound for the last ten months, with strict prohibitions against fraternisation between marines, and sharing a bunk room with three guys, all mean that I've had a dry time of it. The Lunus Two supply transport ship operates with a minimum crew, and so manning it kept us all busy. Since leaving the Oort belt nine months earlier, we've been on a four on, four off, rotation, and as soon as I have a chance to hit my bunk, I have nothing more in mind than sleep, unless it's time to shower or chow down. Mmm, I wouldn't mind chowing down on this hunk in front of me.

Then I remember being told once to never put skin-on-skin with a Zorth. They release some kind of hormone when they're attracted to you, and the galaxy help anyone hit by that erotic cocktail. Does a handshake count? Not like this gorgeous specimen would be attracted to little old me.

With the croakiest voice ever, I tell him, 'I'm E6 Hearn. Jay Hearn. Marine Supply Transport Lunus Two. One of our generators blew. We made it here, just. Sorry to drop in on you like this.'

'Your people are hurt?' His voice sounds like a rock fall, and sends vibrations through my entire body.

With a supreme effort, I pull my focus back to the business in hand. 'Yes. We have seven badly injured marines. Are you able to help?'

The Zorth nods. 'I am Remanvilolemo. My friends call me Lemo. I shall bring help. Wait here.'

Well, with that mouthful, thank Mars he shortens his name. As he turns and strides away, my helmet AI translates rather belatedly, *Remanvilolemo—well endowed.* I almost choke. Seriously? No need to ask where he got that moniker from. More heat pools, and spreads to my girl parts, which grow slick as well as hot. Now is so not the time. I make my way back to E8 and bring him up to speed.

'Good. From now on, you'll be our liaison officer. We're at their mercy right now, so we'd best keep them sweet. Give him anything he wants. And I mean anything.'

Gulp. Did the Master Sergeant really mean *anything*? Not that the big alien would notice a puny human girl like me. Then common sense kicks in, and I realise that E8 probably just meant whatever they might want from our cargo.

Ellery clears his throat and glares at me. Oops, I got so carried away that I forgot to acknowledge his last. 'Yes, Sir.'

He gives me a long look, then lets it go. 'In the meantime, go and help McKeehan and Hickory with the casualties.'

'Yes, Sir. Um, Sir?'

'Proceed.'

'Did we manage to get a distress call out?'

E8 gives me a considering look, then shakes his head. Even if he hadn't decided me to be strong enough to take the news, that look would've given it away. 'The explosion took out our transmitters. Homing beacon's dead.'

'Thank you, Sir.'

At his nod, I spin on my heel and head across the devastation of the bridge and toward the temporary sick bay. At my approach, McKeehan looks up and smiles. 'Good, we need all the help we can get. Would you be kind enough to take over here, Ma'am? Sit with him. Hold his hand.' E4's eyes say all they need to. Nothing more can be done for Bacon. At my nod, McKeehan says, 'Thanks. I'll go see where else I can be useful.'

He shuffles away, and I drop to my knees by the dying E2's side. Bacon has always struck me as a nice guy, and a capable private first class. Blood soaks his chest, and his breathing bubbles horrifically. His eyes lock on mine when I take his hand, and I give it a reassuring squeeze. 'I got you, Bacon. Just rest. Help's on its way.'

'Where … we?' He gasps and wheezes and pain pinches his face.

'Sshh. Save your strength. We're gonna be okay. We landed on Zorth. One of the locals has gone to get us some help.'

Bacon squeezes my hand, then lays back and closes his eyes. We both know he won't make it. Every once in a while, someone lets out a soft moan. The smells of hot metal and melted plastic burn into my nostrils and turn my stomach. Should I talk to him? Or let him go in peace? He answers for me. 'Wife …'

'Yes. I'll go see her myself. You have my word.' *If we ever got off this planet.* Do the Zorths have that kind of technology? I wish I knew more about them.

Bacon's next hand squeeze feels much weaker, and his eyes roll in their sockets. By the time he finds my gaze again, he's gone the colour of spoiled milk, and sweat glistens on his skin. I put my hand to his forehead—cold and clammy. His breath rattles out noisily, and he fails to take another one in. Moments later, his eyes turn glassy. He's gone. With a sigh, I ease his lids closed and drop onto my backside. Did I manage to give him any comfort? With another sigh, I wipe a stray tear from my cheek and then heave to my feet, intending to see if McKeehan can use my help with anyone else. Just then, a commotion at the hole in the hull draws my attention.

Lemo steps through the gap and waves to me. More enormous dark shapes loom behind him. Relieved, I pick my way to him as quickly as the debris and my bruised thigh allow. My knee hurts like hell, and I wonder if I've done more serious damage than I'd initially thought. When I knelt down next to Bacon, something had popped and crunched. With all the meds my suit has pumped into me, though, it will be a while before I feel anywhere near the actual amount of pain I'm in.

I limp up to the alien with a smile. He turns to a darker grey male behind him and speaks. A moment later, my AI provides a translation—*This is the pretty I told you about.* Surprised but pleased, I blush. As I stare up at his chiselled features, his nostrils flare, and he murmurs, 'Vasohamo.' When my AI translates that, I rather wish it hadn't. *Aroused.* He can smell me? Oh Mars. That's all I need. With a smirk, his darker companion moves past him, stretcher in hand. Eight more Zorths follow behind and head for the casualties. Lemo draws me to one side.

'You are hurt?'

'No, it's fine, really—'

He places one of his deliciously thick fingers on my lips. 'I was not asking. You are hurt.'

With that, he stoops, scoops me into his strong arms, and carries me out of the hull. It takes a couple of seconds for me to push through the haze of shock, and I wriggle in his hold. 'Lemo, please. I have to stay. Master Sergeant didn't give me leave to—'

'Your E8 told you to give me anything I want.'

'You heard that? How?'

Lemo grins. 'We have good hearing. So, you do whatever I want, yes?'

Bemused, I can only nod.

'Besides, you are on Zorth now, and your human ranks mean nothing. Here, I am boss.'

'And where're you taking me, *boss*?'

'To Nimanis. She is healer. Will repair you. Then I take you home. Take care of your other need. Yes?'

'M-my other need?' My voice comes out all squeaky.

He stops and stares down at me. In his arms, my face lays against his chest, and one of his hands presses beneath my buttocks. Lemo takes a deep breath in, and when his nostrils flare again, he gives me a grin and strokes my bottom. 'Repair first. Then we join.' Then he plants a quick kiss on my lips and strides onward.

Oh Mars. How in the galaxy will I get out of this one? Yes, I like the man … alien … whatever, but sleep with him? We only just met, and besides, he's huge. My brain provides me with a vivid image of what that gorgeous girth might do to me, and I wriggle some more, so wet now that the crotch of my jumpsuit sticks into my groin. Lemo chuckles and rubs my ass some more, but doesn't pause in his long-legged lope.

All hot and bothered, I relax my head against his hard pecs and nuzzle into his neck. He smells like all spice, with a sexy musky scent beneath it. I can only blame the pain meds my suit's pumped me full of for my relaxed, wanton state. Oh well, maybe I have overdone the skin-on-skin just a tad. Each step jostles me up and down in his arms, and the broad forearm that my butt rests on, rubs me through my jumpsuit.

In this sexed up, drugged up, warm and fuzzy haze, safe and secure in Lemo's arms, I give in to the exhaustion that's been nipping at my consciousness since I came to in the smoke and cacophony of the crash landing. Although he seems to carry me for an age, and the journey feels long, I lose track and have no real sense of distance.

I rouse some time later when lights come into view across the flat, red expanse ahead of us, and Lemo murmurs into my ear, 'Jinazal. Our … how you say? … Capital city. Rest. Not long now.' A few jostles later, my AI translates *Mighty*, and then I slip back into my comforting haze. My last thoughts focus on the Zorths' penchant for naming things literally and honestly. What would Lemo like to name me?—Other than *Jazidal*—pretty. Then I fall down a black hole for a while.

When I next surface, I find myself on a narrow bed, naked and coverless, with my right leg in a hard, white sleeve from groin to toes. A clear tube snakes into my left wrist, with some kind of pink fluid dripping into my vein. Bright white illumination comes from somewhere, although I can't discern any obvious lighting.

Seconds after I open my eyes, the door whooshes open and a female Zorth enters. Her skin holds an azure hue, which enhances her attractive and equally vivid blue eyes. The woman crosses to my bed and gives me a broad smile. 'Ah. You have woken. I am Nimanis. How are you feeling, Jay Hearn?'

If not for the lovely alien's nakedness, I would feel a lot more self-conscious and concerned, but this is obviously normal for them—male and female alike. Before I reply, I do a quick body scan, and aside from the obvious leg injury, I feel fine. I smile and nod and tell her, 'I'm good, thank you. And, please, call me Jay. Hearn is my family name, and only used for formality.'

Nimanis nods. 'Jay, it is my great honour to meet you.'

With a glance down at my encased limb, I ask her, 'How's my leg? Is it badly broken?'

The healer takes my hand and holds it in her much larger and incredibly soft one. Her thumb rubs the back of it while she speaks. 'You had lot of damage. Will take long time to repair. We gave you new knee, and your body will need to grow around it. I am sorry.'

'No, please, thank you. You helped.' I want to ask how long I'll have to stay like this, but I don't want to make her feel like she has to apologise to me again. Without her help, and Lemo, I'd be in a big mess right now. And, best of all, I don't feel any pain at all. And the bed feels soft and supportive beneath me. The room is warm, so despite my nudity, I feel comfortable.

Nimanis nods again, and with a smile, says, 'Get some rest. Soon you will have visitor. I will come see you later.'

While I splutter at the thought of a visitor while I'm lying here exposed, Nimanis disappears through the door again. A frantic glance around the bright room shows it to be as bare as me, with nothing to hand to employ as a temporary aid to my modesty. And with this hard sleeve running the entire length of my leg, I can't go anywhere. I'm utterly stuck. Oh joy. And no useful shadows to hide in either. Who the galaxy is coming to see me?

Only minutes later, I get my answer. The door whooshes open and in strides Lemo, concern clouding his dreamy, dark eyes. He steps to the side of my bed, perches on the edge, and then takes hold of my hand, rubbing the back much like Nimanis did. 'How are you, Jay Hearn?'

With a chuckle, I correct him on the name thing, and then say, 'I'm doing well, Lemo, thank you. And I appreciate you helping me.' Meanwhile, my brain is yammering at me that I'm lying here naked and exposed with a gargantuan, attractive, well endowed male Zorth sitting right next to me. The velvet flesh of his thigh brushes my hip when he shifts to gaze down at me. The tender smile stretching his lips has me go all wobbly.

'I made promise. Repair first.' The rest of his promise lingers in the air between us.

'Um, yes, you did.' What more can I say? In spite of my embarrassment, that flush of excited heat flares low in my belly again, and moisture pools between my legs. I groan because he'll smell it on me. Sure enough, the man's nostrils flare, and his eyes widen. Then he saddens.

'My pretty is not repaired. Will take two moons before.'

His look of dejection brings my sense of humour to the fore, and I tease him, 'Oh, that's a shame.'

He takes me at my word. 'Lemo and Jay Hearn cannot join yet, but I take care of you.'

Oh, um. Yum.

I squirm on the bed. Even though I was joking with him, I do want him. More than I've ever wanted any man in my entire life. And here's this gorgeous Zorth offering to *take care* of me. I must've died in the crash and gone to heaven.

Lemo leans down and brushes his pewter lips over mine.

With my free hand, I reach up and hold him at the base of his ear, and lift my head for another kiss. I so want more where that came from. Rather than feeling vulnerable, now I just feel horny. Bring on the Zorth meat, please. His chest does that deep rumbly thing it did back at the ship, and my insides turn to liquid. Then I burst into flames when he pushes his solid tongue into my mouth. A moan escapes when I part for him, and he rumbles again. It reminds me of a cat's purr, but a million times deeper and sexier.

He starts off with gentle laps at my tongue, then he thrusts in my mouth, while a hand rests on one of my breasts. My nipples spring to attention beneath his ridged thumb pad, and I arch into him as much as I can manage with the high-tech cast thing hindering movement.

Lazily, his smooth palm drifts down my torso until it comes to rest atop my wet curls. I mewl in pleasure and anticipation and need. Even I can smell me now. Lemo pulls out of my mouth and gives me a look hot enough to blister. 'My pretty.' The way he says it sounds so possessive it almost has me coming with no more than a kiss and a caress. And, oh my, that's nothing compared to what happens when he roves his gaze up and down my naked body, with a gleam of pure arousal burning in his eyes.

'Lemo,' I whisper, almost hoarse, and guide his enormous hand between my legs. His eyes don't leave mine while he parts my folds and slips a long, thick finger inside my core. I bend my left leg at the knee and brace my foot against the mattress while I moan in frustration at my inability to rock my hips into his hand. With another deep rumble, he pushes a second finger inside me and slides them back and forth. Then in goes a third, while he circles my engorged clit with his thumb. And, oh galaxies, that velvet skin of his.

I'm so wet, his fingers make sucking sounds as he fucks me with them. The sensations that assail me are both bliss and torture. I could have him do this to me for the rest of my life, and at the same time, I'm desperate to come. An orgasm builds low in my abdomen and shoots white heat into my clit, while the walls of my core clench around him. Lemo thrusts faster and deeper into my wetness. Oh fuck. I'm done for. Everything in me clenches and then explodes. It takes everything I've got to muffle my cries of ecstasy as I come all over his hand. It's so damn sexy the way he watches me the whole time; never once does he take his eyes from mine.

Out of the corner of my eye, I notice something bobbing in the air. A big something. His cock. His glorious, massive cock. My mouth waters. Curse my lack of repair—I need him inside me. Still watching me, Lemo wraps a hand around his shaft and works it. A drop of pre-cum beads on its end and catches the light.

'Bring it here.' I gesture to my mouth.

His chest gives the loudest, deepest rumble so far, and he stands at the edge of the bed for me. I turn my head and take hold of him. He's long and thick and ribbed as fuck. I lick the head and suck him into my mouth bit by bit. He's so big that I don't have all of him in before he's nudging the back of my throat. Oh boy. I hope we're stuck here long enough for me to repair and get the rest of his promise. And if he's as good with his cock as he is with his fingers, I never want to leave. I work him with my hand while I suck on him and lick him with my mouth and tongue. Lemo bucks his hips, and he slips further into me, going deep throat.

At first, I gag a bit but then recover. I'm fine. I can breathe around him as he slides out. And this feels exquisite. His butt clenches, and he works hard not to go at my face. Instead, he stands rock still and lets me work him in and out. I grip his buttocks and take him as deep as I can. Lemo loses his iron control and thrusts into me with a deep moan. His big hands cradle the back of my head as he rocks in and out of me, and I open as wide as I can for him, keeping my tongue flat so he can slide over it. Just when I think I can't take anymore, he stills and holds me against him. His hot seed pours down my throat, and I swallow until he's done.

I've given plenty of blow jobs before now, but I've never let a guy finish in my mouth before. I never liked the taste, but oh my, his cream is so delicious. I ease him out of my mouth and lick him clean of every last drop. 'My pretty,' he growls out, then drops to his knees by the bed and pulls me in for a kiss.

We lie together, with him knelt on the floor and draped over my upper body, taking care not to smother me or catch my leg or drip. Lemo peppers kisses on my forehead and cheeks and lips. Who knew that recuperating in a medical cot could be so much fun? Satiated, with a smile on my lips, I drift into a light doze.

The whoosh of the door rouses me, and I blink awake to see E8 standing in the doorway with wide-eyed shock and pinkening cheeks. I wonder what the matter is, as Lemo is nowhere to be seen, and then I remember my nakedness. Funny how quickly I adjusted when it was just the Zorth and me. Now, in the face of my sergeant's embarrassment, I feel exposed and vulnerable again.

With no other options, I pretend this is all as normal as could be. 'Hi, Sarge. How are you?'

Ellery's poker face drops into blessed place, and he says, 'I'm well, Hearn. Glad to hear you're on the mend. Might be some time, they tell me.'

I nod. 'Two moons. However long that is?'

With his gaze fixed somewhere above my head, E8 confirms, 'Yes, I believe that's about three Earth months or thereabouts.'

'Uh, that long, huh?'

'Yes. Sorry about that, Staff Sergeant. Nothing for it, I'm afraid.'

I nod and lay quietly for a second or two.

E8 breaks the silence, 'Their leader, Remanvilolemo, seems quite taken with you. Good job there, with the liaison business. … Has he made any demands yet? Said what they want in return for helping us?'

I smother a smile. 'Not in so many words, Sir.'

Ellery raises his eyebrows.

'He and Nimanis have been kind and … attentive.'

E8 shoves his hands behind his back and says, 'Good, good. Well, I'd best be off then. I'll check up on you now and again. And, um, see if I can't rustle you up some fresh fatigues.'

'Thank you, Sir.'

It's a relief when the whoosh of the door signals that he's gone and I'm alone again. Funny, but I felt so much more awkward with a fellow human, and a man I've known for years, than I have at any point with either of the Zorth.

At some point, the healer brings me a bowl of creamy broth that reminds me of Lemo's cum. Nimanis sees my flushed cheeks and checks my temperature, even though I try to assure her that I'm okay. Along with the ambrosia, she brings a set of dark green fatigues. 'From your Benjamin Ellery.' A frown draws her brows together. 'How will we get them on you?'

We both look at the huge cast. As much as I quite like the freedom being uncovered gives me, I ask, 'Do you have scissors?'

Nimanis doesn't understand, so I scissor my fingers, and then she nods. 'Ah yes … Nasisalas … *scissors* … yes, will go get.'

When she returns, I talk her through cutting off the pant leg on the right side of the jumpsuit. In the end, we have to make a slit to open up the whole right side. That's the only way we can slide the garment over my body, as no way can I lift or wriggle to get it beneath me. Draped over my torso isn't great, but better than nothing at all, if I have to be covered up for the sake of my fellow humans. Nimanis purses her lips and tells me she will think on a solution.

The next day, when E8 returns, I apologise for wrecking the suit, but he tells me it is no matter, and that when I'm up and on my feet, he's sure they can dig me up another one.

'Sir. Have you managed to contact base?'

He scowls. 'Yes. Had a dickens of an argument with that Vilolemo fellow, but he allowed it eventually. I thought he'd never see sense. Unbelievable, but I'm sure the man expected us to stay here, with them. Anyway, we should have a transport coming this way in about four months.' He gives me a bright smile. 'Just in time to have you back up and on your feet, eh?'

I force a return smile. 'Yes, Sir.'

Inside, something just curled up and died. I'm crushed. I'd hoped that we were stuck here. For certain, I don't want to go back to the life I had before the crash. Military life is a lonely one, and being stuck on supply transports is mind numbing. Back home, I have no family waiting for me, and no friends to speak of. The many wars and planetary skirmishes took anyone I ever got close to until I learned better. Just when I'd convinced myself that being alone was safer and less painful, I met Lemo.

Sure, we haven't spoken much—spent most of our time engaged in other activities—but we connected. When he looked into my eyes while he made me come, it felt like he touched my soul. In fact, every time the door whooshes, I hold my breath and pray that it's him. Ellery eventually shuffles out of the room, and not two minutes later, Lemo comes in. He must've been waiting for the Master Sergeant to leave.

Despite giving him my brightest smile, he sees straight through it and dashes to my side. 'You are hurt?'

'Just sad.'

He takes my hand and perches on the edge of the cot. I'm not sure what the fabric is that forms its mattress, but it seems to self-clean, which obviates the need for sheets. And it feels similar to the Zorth skin. Lemo gives me a tender caress with his eyes. 'Tell me what I can do.'

I sigh. Shake my head. It's no good—I have to leave when the unit does, otherwise they'll class me as a deserter and hunt me down. Worse still, I just know that if it came to that, Lemo and the Zorth would protect me, even if that meant going to war with the coalition. No amount of booty is worth another Intergalactic war.

Damn this medication they have me on—it's destroyed my usual defences, and a tear slips down my cheek even while I continue to smile and say, 'It's okay, Lemo, really. Just life.'

My big grey alien leans in and kisses the salty wetness away, then settles on my lips. Hungry, I deepen the kiss and his embrace changes from comforting to passionate. Our tongues tangle together, and his hands roam. The first thing he does is to pull off my jumpsuit and shove the garment down to my left ankle, out of the way.

He pulls out of the kiss to watch me. 'You want Lemo take care of you?'

I nod. 'Mmm, that would be so good.'

Because I expect him to use his hands on me like before, his next move surprises me. Lemo scoots to the bottom of the cot and eases my left leg over his broad shoulder, then dips his head between my legs and nuzzles at my already-dripping folds. I got aroused as soon as he walked into the room. My soft sigh of satisfaction morphs into an excited gasp when he licks me from front to rear and back again. A rumble erupts from his chest. When he thrusts his thick tongue into me, I almost lift off the bed, and only the cast keeps me anchored.

Lemo rests his hands on my hips and fucks me with his tongue. When he fails to come up for air, I reckon the Zorth must be able to breathe through their ears—either that, or he's skilled at free diving. Whatever, no complaints coming from this gal.

Just moans and mewls while he makes me come.

He doesn't stop until I lay limp and utterly spent beneath him, then he kisses his way up my body and claims my lips with his. Okay, shoot me now, 'cos I just fell in love with this alien … man … sex god. What will I do when the relief transporter turns up to snatch us away? I wrap my arms around Lemo's shoulders and pull him in tight.

The guy is in my head, I swear. He tells me, 'Your E8 contacted your people. I want keep you.'

I hold my breath.

'But Zorth do not force their mates. Jay Hearn must choose.'

I smile at the way he says my name. It's growing on me. 'I want to stay,' I say in a small voice, then clear my throat. 'The coalition military won't let me go, though. I have a contract with them. It means I have to go with them when they come.'

Lemo shakes his head. 'We will sort out.'

I hug him even more fiercely. 'Thank you, but I don't want to start any wars.'

He chuckles and nuzzles my neck. 'I am Zorth leader. Your E8 tells you give me what I want. Lemo wants Jay Hearn. Settled. That is that.'

I have to laugh. What I wouldn't give to see E8's face when he hears that little speech. Still, worry gnaws at me. Everything depends upon E8 and his superiors going for it. And I'm not sure they will. It smacks of kidnap, and the coalition doesn't trade with terrorists or hold any truck with blackmailers. Nope, we need a stronger bargaining chip. Mmm.

Lemo chuckles against my neck, then lifts to look at me. 'My pretty has great engines thrumming in her head.' The smile he gives me is proud and possessive. 'My Jay Hearn is clever and knows what humans will want.'

He leans down and kisses me thoroughly. I reach out and take hold of his thick length. Time for a protein dessert.

The days follow on one after another in much the same manner, with Lemo visiting me as often as he can. We share pleasure and conversation, and Lemo teaches me the Zorthian language. The days become weeks, which grow into months. I mull over what can't be done. Or can it? I wonder. It might work.

Nimanis comes to me after lunch, wearing a big smile. 'Today, we remove leg medicine.'

With a squeal of delight, I grab my favourite alien (second only to Lemo) and give her a fierce hug. The woman laughs and sets about disconnecting the drip. Next, Nimanis removes the sheet from me. It's made from sewn together fatigues, and Lemo told me that my fellow marines made it for me. I still can't picture all those big, masculine guys all sitting in a sewing circle without creasing up. The healer goes to a panel on the wall and presses a button. A series of beeps and clicks follow, then a hiss startles me when the cast splits open down its middle.

Because the leg has been sealed in the cast for so long, I grimace, expecting the foul stench of unwashed, shrivelled flesh to greet me. Nimanis hovers near. 'It hurts?'

'No. I thought it would be all gross because I haven't been able to clean it …'

'Ah, Jay has much to learn about Zorth.'

'I can't wait,' I tell her with the biggest grin I've ever worn.

My leg looks as good as new—better, even. And the muscles are strong and useable. I'd expected a long time of rehab and having to rebuild my strength. Not so. Somehow, not only did the machine keep my limb clean, it also kept the muscles working. Likewise, when Nimanis helps me into a sitting position, I wait for dizziness to hit after being horizontal for so long. None comes. Full of anticipation, I allow the alien to help me regain my feet. I can't believe it … after three months stuck on the cot, I'm walking around like I never lost my feet in the first place. Only the impending arrival of the transport ship spoils my joy.

The healer knows just how to cure my melancholy, though, and walks me away from the only room I've known since we landed here and toward a private suite of rooms in an accommodation wing. And if the sight of the luxurious surroundings isn't enough to fill me with happiness, then the discovery of Lemo in my new bedroom is. With a low chuckle, Nimanis leaves us to it.

My man rises from the large bed and reaches me in two strides. Then he pulls me into his arms, and in a fierce voice that turns me to jelly, tells me, 'Now we join.'

In one swift move, he scoops me into his arms, turns, and flings me onto the waiting bed. The mattress bounces beneath me, and I giggle when I see his pouch retract to reveal just how big and bad my gorgeous Zorth is. Thanks to the makeshift bed cover being left in the hospital room, I've arrived here nice and nude. Nimanis, for some reason, forgot to bring the spare jumpsuit that E8 promised. I'll have to be sure to thank her.

Lemo drops onto the bed by my side and props on his elbows, where he lays looking at me for the longest time. My heart melts. Enough tenderness and passion lace his gaze that he doesn't need to lay a finger on me to have me desperate for him.

My long incarceration has given us plenty of time and opportunity to explore one another—front and back, and top to bottom. We've discovered what we like, what we're indifferent about, and what has us coming quicker than you can blink. With a grin, I reach up and stroke the base of Lemo's skull, which seems to be a g-spot for the Zorth. Chest rumbling, he mashes his hot lips on mine and claims me with his tongue.

My nipples rub against the velvet of his chest and

immediately pebble. Just that small touch drives me wild, and wetness floods my folds. Lemo plunders me with his thrusting tongue and covers me with his large, firm body. His hot, hard shaft nudges against my thigh. I part for him, and he slides along my wet lips as our hips rock together. My pussy clenches, ready for him, but he doesn't give me the satisfaction I crave, not yet—even though he wants to plunge into me every bit as much as I want him filling me.

Lemo teases me with a couple more slides along my aching folds, then kisses his way down my body, his lips searing my skin as he goes. This time, when he circles my clit with his hot, thick tongue, I'm free to arch into him, craving more. His groans tickle my engorged nub, and my hips buck against his face. With a grunt and a rumble, he invades my inner walls with his tongue while sliding his hands beneath my buttocks and lifting me into him. Every nerve in my body tingles as he fucks me with his tongue and glides his fingers back and forth, dragging my moisture to my tight, puckered back entrance. On the next slick glide, he plunges a finger inside me, and I gasp in ecstasy. I feel deliciously full when he pushes it all the way in, and when he bends it a little and hits just the spot, I writhe against him, wild with passion. I've never felt anything so erotic. Lemo synchronises his rhythm with tongue and finger and plunders me again and again until I can't take any more. I beg him, 'Lemo, please.'

His only response is to tongue fuck me harder, faster, and deeper until I scream his name while a white-hot release tears through me. Not giving me chance to catch my breath, Lemo takes hold of his cock and positions himself at my entrance. I need him inside me. Now. Right fucking now. 'Lemo, please.'

At my plea, the big bad alien pauses and snares my gaze. His eyes smoulder and burn a hole right through my core. My juices drip from his mouth and glisten on his chin. Oh my. With the slightest twitch of his hips, he teases me with the head of his cock just inside me. 'Lemo, please. I need you … now.'

I push my groin into his, trying to encourage him to spear me, but he stills me with firm hands and demands, 'Tell me what you want.' Then he bends in half and nibbles one of my nipples. I feel empty when his shaft moves away from me, and a moan of protest bursts free from my throat. Lemo just chuckles and gives the other nipple a nip, before giving them both a soothing lick of his tongue.

'I want you inside me. Now.'

A wicked grin lifts his lips when he pushes back to my entrance and holds there. 'What is your human word? Tell me what you want me to do.'

Is it possible for a body to endure more frustration? I almost growl at him, 'Fuck me. Fuck me now, Remanvilolemo.'

My use of his full name seems to set him on fire, and he pushes inside me. I gasp as I feel the stretch. He's long and wide and oh so fucking hot. It burns a little, and I tense. Lemo pauses to let the sting fade, and invades my mouth with his tongue. Then he eases in further, before pulling back until he rests just inside me. Oh Mars, if the galaxy gods are listening, please let me die now. This is too much. I gasp. 'Please.'

Lemo bites down on my bottom lip, and then thrusts all the way in. His girth stretches me to the full, and he hits every goddam g-spot I have. 'Oh my God,' I cry as I rock against him. His hands grip my buttocks and squeeze as he pummels me. Damn him, though—he's being too careful with me. I need him to take me completely. 'Harder, faster, now.'

I'm rewarded with a low rumble from his gorgeous chest, which has me squirting more juices around him and clenching, even as he obeys my commands and hammers into me. Sweat slicked and heart pounding, I roll my hips and meet his thrusts, getting maximum penetration. Lemo pins my hands above my head and drops his head to the pillow beside me, while he fucks me with wild abandon. Each thrust so powerful that it drives me up the mattress until my head knocks against the (mercifully) padded headboard every time he drives into me.

And still I need more. My walls clench around him, and I dig my nails into his shoulders, while I gasp and beg. Then the orgasm hits me, blinding in its intensity. Lemo pummels me while I scream and buck beneath him, lost in sheer pleasure. Then he stiffens on top of me, and hot heat fills my core. 'You're mine,' he snarls out as his cock pulses and spurts inside me. He keeps thrusting until he's completely empty, and we both collapse to the bed, spent and content.

After a short while, he shrinks and slips from me, and then Lemo rolls to my side and pulls me into his warm embrace. I fall asleep to the beat of his heart while his lips nuzzle into my hair.

For the rest of the afternoon and the whole night through, we find pleasure in one another. Sometimes making long, slow love, and others fucking each other into oblivion. Only for short bursts do we doze, entangled together, before one of us rouses the other for another go.

I have to love Zorth technology. When my stomach rumbles me awake in the morning, Lemo leaps out of bed and crosses to a hatch in the far wall. With the simple press of a few buttons, a feast arrives, and he brings the tray of delights to the bed. We start off feeding one another, and end up devouring more than just the food.

A couple of hours later, I finally stagger into the shower, somewhat bowlegged and wearing a silly grin. Lemo follows me into the hot spray, and shows me how inventive he can be with the shower head. The stamina of the Zorth is mind blowing. Eventually, he has to go and do some leading, while I have to go and find E8 so I can lay out the plan that's been fermenting all this time.

I may have found a solution, and hopefully the coalition will go for it. It feels like a gargantuan task ahead of me, for not only do I need to get E8 on side, I also need to convince the Zorth and the men who hold the galaxy in the palms of their hands. They'll either support my idea or crush it in their fists.

From my closet, I retrieve a new set of fatigues, and then go in search of my Sergeant Major. The stiff cotton rasps against my raw nipples and chaffed pussy with every step, but rather than being unpleasant, it brings me to fresh arousal. I have to bite my cheek hard to stop myself from turning around and going after Lemo instead. I tell myself, 'Come on, girl. You have to do this.'

Ellery, McKeehan, and Hickory sit in a common area, playing cards. An open door on the far wall reveals a bunk room. Seems I'm the only one of us that's been given her own quarters, and by the looks of it, rather luxurious ones to boot. Grin firmly stifled, I edge into the room and get E8's attention.

McKeehan and Hickory give me nods and waves, and then make themselves scarce so I can talk with the boss. At his nod, I drop into a chair on the opposite side of the table.

'You're looking well, Hearn.'

'Thank you, Sir. Never been better.'

'Glad to hear it.'

Ellery fixes his steely gaze onto me, and I squirm a little in my seat. I've been so busy thinking about the bigger picture, I forgot about the small detail of opening the damn conversation in the first place. E8 saves me any further trouble, but brings plenty of cringe instead. 'We came looking for you. Their healer said you'd been released, but weren't to be disturbed. Seems you've been spending quite a bit of time with Vilolemo.'

It's none of his business, not until I'm officially back on active duty, which I'm not yet. Not until he says I am, and I hope to forestall that if I can. With a swallow, I firm my shoulders. At least his words have given me a lead in. 'Sir. I need to speak with you about Leader Remanvilolemo.'

The sarge mirrors my stiff posture and stares at me. A tacit instruction to proceed.

'When we landed, you ordered me to give him whatever he wanted.'

E8 nods, lips pursed. He's a shrewd man, and I have to tread carefully here.

'Seems he wants a certain human woman.' I deliberately avoid referring to myself as a staff sergeant. Best dance around that for as long as possible. I don't want to remind him that I'm officially coalition property for the next six years.

Ellery nods again, and his face pinches, telling me his patience is thin and that I'd better get to the point. 'From what I've seen of the Zorth, it would appear that my duties of Liaison Officer could be expanded, to the benefit of all parties.'

Interest lights his eyes, and he sits up straighter in his chair, all attention.

'While I'm certain that the Zorth would never consider a military alliance, it's my belief that they would be open to negotiations pertaining to trade, and supply routes through their system.'

E8 rubs his chin, then pins me with his eyes. 'And why would you volunteer yourself, Hearn?'

I've given this some thought, as I'd expected the question at some point. While to admit my feelings goes against my every instinct, I'm sure that Ellery already knows (or at least suspects) and he won't appreciate it if I try to play him.

'I want to stay, Sarge. I've grown fond of the Zorth.' He raises his eyebrows, so I add, 'More specifically, their leader.'

Ellery nods, so I push onward. Even though I think he's interested, my heart pounds at my ribs. This is a long shot, and I'm all too aware of that. 'The Zorth know me and respect me. And I feel that I could be in an ideal position to negotiate on behalf of … interested parties.' I'd almost said *humans*, but remembered at the last moment that the coalition holds far more interests than merely Earth's. We scrawny bipeds are but a small cog in a vast and universal machine.

We talk for a further half-hour, and then I reach a point where I think I've said more than enough. E8 agrees to contact base and forward my proposition. Now I just have to convince Lemo to go with it, too. Doubts assail me while I retrace my steps to my suite. Did I misread the things he's said to me over the last months? Or has wishful thinking clouded my judgement? It might have been better to approach him before Ellery, but I needed to know whether the sarge would even agree to putting the suggestion forward first.

I don't have to wait long to find out, as Lemo strides into my room about twenty minutes after I get back. Even while the door glides shut behind him, his pouch retracts and shows me how pleased he is to see me. My cheeks flush, and my body responds with heat and moisture, but I clamp my thighs together and tell him we need to talk.

It's difficult to form a coherent sentence when he insists on nuzzling my neck and unzipping my jumpsuit while I talk.

Stubborn girl that I am, I persist despite his best efforts. As I lay it all out for him, he nods and grunts whenever I pause, which is all encouraging. Then he gives me his seal of approval by burying his head between my legs.

Between pussy melting licks, he tells me, 'The Zorth have wanted this for a long time—' More mind-unwinding lathes of his tongue. '—But none of the coalition Ambassadors are trustworthy—' Brain-boiling sucking and nibbling. '—Their word is not worth piss—' He thrusts his tongue into me. And then I'm coming. Lemo gives his full attention to my galaxy-shattering orgasm and licking up as much of my juice as he can.

When I stop writhing and screaming, he slides his ripped body between my thighs, until my knees are over his shoulders and I'm exposed to his hot, hard cock, which he eases into my waiting pussy. With long, slow, tantalising strokes, he carries on the conversation like there's been no interruption. Between moaning quietly and nibbling his earlobe, I manage to engage my brain enough to listen.

'You have met many of our people—' Lemo penetrates me slow but hard. Ungh. Exquisite torture. '—I made a point of introducing you to the Zorth council. You—' Another slow, deep, toe-curling thrust. 'You, baby, they can't help but love.' Then the sensation of slow-fucking me proves too much, and he bites down on my shoulder while he comes at me hard and fast.

I wrap my legs around his hips and squeeze him into me as tightly as I can. Still riding high from his thorough tonguing, a second orgasm isn't far away. Again and again, he hammers into my wet pussy, and I suck him in with greed. Then my vision tunnels, and a scream rips from my throat as waves of pleasure rock my world. My walls clench around him as I come over and over, and then he's yelling 'Jay Hearn!' and spilling into me while he shoves into me again and again. What seems like eons later, we both fall back to Zorth, and tangle together while our breathing settles.

The transport ship is only days away now, but I no longer care. I get to stay. The coalition, always greedy for more goods, more money, more reach, snatched at my proposal. Of course, they tried to switch me out for someone within their control, but the Zorths wouldn't even entertain the shadow of a shadow of a suggestion. So, here I am, no longer a marine but an Ambassador, growing a mini-Lemo in my belly. My big bad alien is over the moons, and refuses to leave my side.

Every time I make even the smallest progress for the Zorth nation, Lemo rewards me with his body. In fact, any time I please him at all, he puts something between my legs. And, much as I love what he can do with his hands and mouth, nothing can match what he achieves with that big, ridged cock.

The day comes to wave goodbye to my shipmates. The transport brings representatives from many nations, and I drive a hard bargain at the negotiating table. Everyone wants to get as much as they can for as little as possible. Thing is, I'm not playing ball. Zorth is rich in minerals and fine metals, not to mention their awesome technology, which all puts them in a strong position, and I make the most of this. By the time the transport takes the delegates away again, along with the surviving marines, I've secured firm promises from every single planet that sent a representative, and I've tied up the coalition so tightly that they can't wriggle or manoeuvre. In short, I have everyone where I want them, and that's in a position that's fair and generous for everybody.

As soon as the ship clears the take-off pad, Lemo picks me up in those wonderful strong arms of his and carries me to our quarters. By the time he places me on the bed, I'm wet and ready and panting for him. I won't last long, and judging by the bead of moisture at the end of his shaft, neither will he. His velvet skin nudges my thighs open wide as he settles between my legs and sets about showing me just how well I've done.

If this is my reward, I'll make sure to keep on doing such a good job. It sure beats anything the coalition can offer.

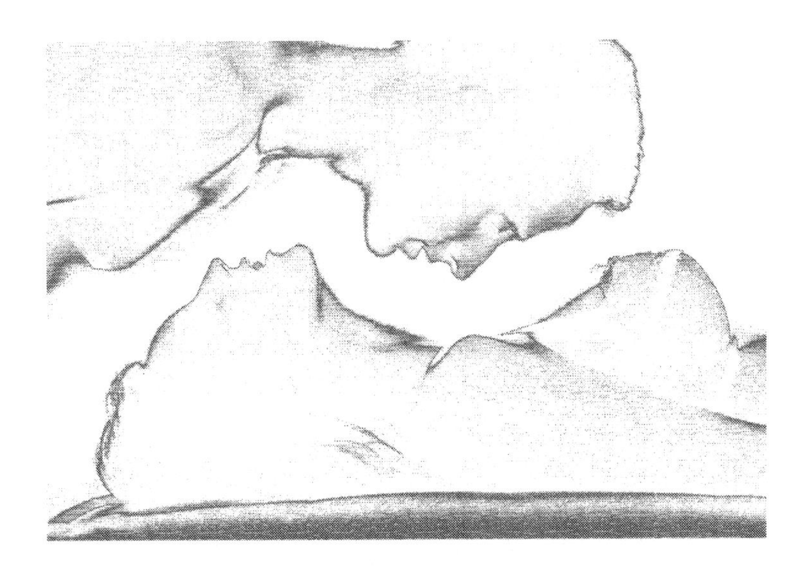

CHAPTER TEN

Saving Face

Dr Waverley looked up at the knock on the door, an impatient frown darkening his face. Try as he might, he still hadn't managed to find the article he needed. Ten medical journals already poured over, and at least as many again to wade through. Nurse Pritchett, a chit of a girl, stood framed in the doorway, wringing her hands with nerves.

Dr Waverley slipped a marker into the book to keep the page, and then held the frail yet attractive nurse's stare. 'Well? What is it, girl?'

She smoothed her hands on her starched white apron. 'Doctor. A lady to see you.'

'What lady? For goodness sakes.'

'A-a Lady Alfred Jones, Sir.'

The doctor failed to recognise the name and his mouth turned down even further. 'What does she want?'

The nurse looked positively terrified by now, and kept glancing over her shoulder. 'She, she would have you perform surgery, Doctor.'

He rubbed at his forehead in an effort to produce some

patience for this dense girl. Did she not know the routine for these kinds of solicitations by now? 'Send her to see one of the juniors. If they see fit, they'll ask me to see her. Take down her details and give her the forms to fill in.'

Nurse Pritchett stood there, mouth working soundlessly.

'Well, that will be all.' More annoyed than ever, he retrieved the book. A shadow darkened the room a little, and the doctor looked up again, ready to berate the idiotic creature. However, a lady had taken the nurse's place. A lady he recognised in the flesh if not in the name.

She smiled. 'Doctor Waverley, how nice to see you. It's been a long time.'

Her careful formality hurt. Flustered, he let the book go once more, arose, and motioned the woman to enter the room. Once she'd done so, he closed the door and retook his seat. Annalise Cheviot—aka Lady Alfred Jones—lowered her graceful form into the chair in front of his desk.

'To what do I owe the pleasure?' He had to ask out of politeness' sake, despite the obvious apparatus sitting on her face. If the tinted eyeglasses didn't give it away, the fake nosepiece most certainly did. Shock cooled his veins and robbed him of sense for a second or two. Ladies, in his experience, didn't normally succumb to diseases more accustomed to making the acquaintance of whores. The doctor didn't need to see beneath the apparatus to know that Annalise bore a syphilitic nose—or, more accurately, bore a hole where that nose would once have been. How far gone was she? Apart from the apparatus, she seemed in good health and fair spirits, and the blue devils didn't seem to have sunk their claws into her.

Lady Jones sat in silence and let him muse, and only when he'd caught her eye and flushed upon realising he had been staring, did she speak to him. 'As you can see, Doctor, I am in need of some assistance.'

He shook his head, wishing to demure. 'I am not the physician you need, my lady. Doctor Broderick—a good man and a good friend, a brick—is far more experienced at dealing with … such ailments.'

A sad smile nudged Annalise's lips, but got lost in her pale cheeks long before it reached anywhere near her eyes. 'I can trust no one else. Only you. Time and again, you have proven to be an honest and honourable man. Please, Sir, don't turn me away in my hour of greatest need.'

'What of your husband?' The question broke free before he could edit it. Soften it. Make it less blunt.

If the question left her uncomfortable, she hid it well. 'Ah, yes. And that leads us to the heart of the matter.'

The doctor's eyes widened. Did she mean to say that Lord Alfred Jones had given her this awful malady? Surely not. But then, that would be better than any alternative he might conjure.

Annalise leant forward a little in her seat. 'May I ask that you permit me to tell you a story?'

The glasses she wore made it impossible to read her eyes, and so, much of her demeanour escaped him just yet. This woman intrigued him. Why seek him out after five years without communication or contact of any sort? And, with such a delicate problem, why ask him when any number of physicians in the city could assist? Perturbed yet curious, he nodded.

Annalise leant back, gave a dainty clearing of her throat, and then said, 'May I further ask your indulgence in suffering the repetition of some information of which you may already be aware?'

The physician placed his hands in his lap, beneath the desk, and said, 'Please, Lady Jones, proceed.'

Before saying anything further, the still-pretty young woman removed her hat and gloves and placed them on the far corner of the table. Then, after smoothing her hands down her voluminous dress (of the latest fashion), she claimed his gaze with those piercing hazel eyes of hers. 'Firstly, please would you accept my apology?'

'No apology needed.'

A glint of amusement brightened her eyes. 'Once, a certain young gentleman told me that he would brook no refusal. That he was, in fact, deaf to such shenanigans. Let me now offer that refusal to you.'

'Very well. Apology accepted. Continue.' He gestured for her to get a move on; impatient to hear what she had to say. The medical journal stole his attention repeatedly, and so he snatched it up and stuffed it into the drawer of his desk in the hope that out of sight would, in this instance, mean out of mind.

'I repeat some aspects of my story with which you may be familiar in an attempt to convey my perspective to the scene. I feel … it is important, Sir, that you understand how it is that I came to my current condition.'

'My lady, it is neither my business nor my concern.'

'Still …'

'In that case, tea is in order. Tea and nibbles. Please, excuse me a moment.' The doctor rose from his seat and went in search of a nurse. He found the sweet-faced Miss Bernard. She looked doe-eyed and innocent, but just the other evening she'd blown his flute in his office while the rest of the night-shrouded hospital settled to sleep. He twitched inside his trousers at the recollection. After conveying his request, he returned to his office and Lady Jones.

The two talked of inconsequential matters until Nurse Bernard brought a tray of tea and dainties. The girl placed the ornate silver tray on the sideboard and set about pouring. As soon as she'd done, Doctor Waverley thanked her and sped her on her way. The wall lamp, fed by that newfangled electricity the hospital had only just had installed, flickered and buzzed. The good doctor glanced at it with suspicion. Innovation was overrated.

Annalise sipped at her tea, and then placed the cup back in its saucer while holding his gaze. Attention secured, she took them for a stroll down memory lane.

⚜

Annalise's father turned a severe face to her and repeated, 'I shall brook no argument. You shall come out at tonight's ball, and tomorrow, we shall announce your engagement. My decision is final.'

Head bowed, the girl replied, 'Yes, Papa.' Despite her apparent agreement, her heart had no intention of following her tongue. The man was an old buffer—at least forty, and nothing to look at despite his penchant for dandy attire. Within ten minutes of their introduction the day previous, boredom had driven Annalise to distraction. Next to David, Mr Jones brought to mind stale bread and soured milk. Whereas *him*?—He recalled roses and frolicking and all things fun in the world.

Quietly, he had courted her, and only waited to make an official arrangement because she hadn't yet come out. Then there was the added matter of him being her stepbrother. Though they bore no blood relation to one another, him being the son of her father's second wife, her papa would suffer apoplexy if he knew their affections to be more than those of siblings.

The fact of his being seen as her brother had allowed them many more liberties than a young lady of her station would ordinarily have had opportunity of. Attentive as he'd been, not once had he made improper advances; although, on more than one occasion, he had been visibly excited when in solitary company with her.

She resolved to find a way to speak with him in private that very night. There must be a way to slip away from the party unobserved for a time.

The hours dragged by, and then it came time for Annalise to suffer the ministrations of Betsy, her lady's maid, and her stepmother while they transformed her from the wild, wilful girl she'd hitherto been into a beautiful, decorous young debutante. Actually, not so young. They'd delayed her coming out because of her mother's death and the requisite period of mourning. Then had come her father's engagement and remarriage, which had further postponed things. At nineteen, she was positively an old maid. Still, joy thrilled her when she twirled in front of the mirror that evening.

Her new gown flowed around her and gave the impression of floating rather than walking. In the latest Parisian fashion, it gathered beneath her chest and draped in voluptuous folds down her torso and limbs. To be unbound and corsetless, felt liberating. On the cusp of becoming a debutante, Annalise wore her blonde tresses in an up do, and wouldn't wear it down in public anymore. A sure sign that her girlish days were done with.

'A vision,' Betsy told her with a proud smile.

'You'll do,' her stepmother said with a look of cold appraisal. 'It's not as if you haven't already made a good match. Come, let us away. We mustn't keep the guests waiting.'

Annalise paused at the head of the stairs, her closed fan held in trembling fingers—filled with anticipation and not a little trepidation. From the midst of the throng, warm brown eyes snatched her breath away and claimed her focus. David. On the arm of her stepmother, she made her careful way down the broad, curved stairway.

A tedium of introductions followed, and then dances with men that held no interest for her whatsoever. At last, at long last, brother and sister secured each other's arms as the band struck up the Viennese Waltz. An old number, for the times, but so typical of her papa and stepmother to include in the itinerary. At least it gave them an excuse to hold one another that not even society's most proper could frown at.

When the dance wound to a close, Annalise took David's arm and led him to the refreshment room, before some other man could claim her company. All at once, a brief and unexpected bonus came their way. Only the two of them occupied the room. The double doors stood open to let in the summer breeze from the gardens. Quickly, before anyone could witness their dash for freedom, Annalise grabbed David's hand and pulled him into the garden. 'I must speak with you,' she said when he hesitated to come with.

On silent yet swift feet, she led him away from the lights and toward the darkness of the distant arbour. When they reached it, she sank with relief onto the marble bench along its far wall. A giggle bubbled out of her when David, panting, flopped down next to her. Her mirth soon evaporated when he asked her whatever the matter was.

'Oh, my sweet. Papa has decided I am to be married. To a banker. He refused to hear any demurral from me. What are we to do?'

Silent, visibly upset, he took her hand in his and squeezed. 'We must confess our affections. I can see no other way.'

'Oh, my love!' Annalise threw her arms around his neck and hugged him.

Initially, he stiffened, but after a second, melted into her embrace and nuzzled into her neck. The move caused her breath to hitch, and she pulled back enough to look at him. David took the opportunity to brush a soft kiss over her lips, which set her heart to skipping. He'd never touched her in this way before.

When he lifted away, Annalise leaned in and kissed him in return. He increased the pressure and placed a hand at the back of her neck. His tongue lapped at the seam of her lips, and carried away on the wings of passion, she opened for him. All thought of meek propriety fled before the inflamed beast.

Their tongues tangled together, and he moaned into her mouth. He tasted spicy, with a hint of cinnamon—no doubt from the supper he'd imbibed just a little earlier. His manly musk only served to further arouse her, and she held onto his shoulders and pushed her chest into his.

New sensations assailed her and stole her senses. Heat coiled low in her belly, and a soft whimper escaped her lips. David placed a hand on her upper arm, which felt nowhere near enough. Annalise pulled away so she could speak. 'Put your hands on me.' Her daring words sent a flash of thrill through her.

When he hesitated, she took his hand and placed it on her heaving bosom, just above the low neckline. Now he grew eager, and plunged his tongue into her once again, while fondling her breast. Dampness settled between her thighs, and Annalise dropped a hand to his lap—intending to rest it on his upper thigh. Her aim misjudged, however, and instead came to rest on something hard.

Startled, she lifted her hand away, but David guided it back and encouraged her to stroke it. With more moans of pleasure, they tumbled backward onto the wide bench, and his hard length pressed into her through their clothing. The ministrations of his tongue drove her wild, and then he reached behind and found the hem of her gown. A shudder rippled up her spine when he slipped his hand beneath the long skirt and caressed his way up her shin, over her knee, and along her thigh.

Annalise writhed beneath him, no longer damp but soaking wet, and her hips rocked into his groin. He rubbed himself against her, and disengaged from her lips. For a moment, she felt empty without him, but then he lowered his mouth to her breast, which he teased out of her gown with his other hand, and then sucked into his mouth.

Shock jolted her; a lady didn't allow such a thing, but they *were* to marry, so that was all right, wasn't it? When his tongue lathed her nipple, it was like nothing she'd ever experienced before. A cry burst forth, and lust chased her reservations away. It seemed like the pleasure went straight from her breast to the warm wet place between her legs.

David freed her other nipple and gave it the same attention, while he moved his hand from her thigh and eased it into her underwear. For the second time that evening, Annalise thanked the fashion-gods for favouring smaller and simpler. Where he wanted to be, he parted her folds with a finger and dipped it into her entrance by a fraction.

Her hips bucked wildly, and more of her cream slicked her and coated his digit. He worked it around in a circle, and the sensations overwhelmed her. Doubts nudged the edges her of her awareness, but Annalise remained entirely focused on the exquisite tingling of her nerve endings. Then his thumb found and rubbed the little nub just above her secret place. His mouth sought hers, and he invaded her with his tongue, while she writhed and moaned beneath him.

His erection pressed into her belly, and he lifted his mouth to say, 'You can touch me too, you know.'

With an embarrassed giggle, she squirmed her hand between them and squeezed him through the thin cloth of his trousers. He disengaged to unfasten his pants and free himself, and then wrapped her hand around his hot, hard shaft. Her fingertips barely met, he was so thick. Satisfied, he returned his hand to the junction of her thighs, and continued to tease her with his fingers.

Once in a while, he ceased his kisses to instruct her on how best to work her hand up and down his cock. Moisture pooled at its end and coated her fingers as she glided over his slit and back down his length.

The more her passion grew, the faster she stroked. Every muscle in her body tensed and contracted, ready for a release that must surely come soon. Expert fingers gave exquisite torture as they stroked her nub and made frequent, teasing border intrusions into her entrance. Through the fog of desire, Annalise registered and appreciated that he took care not to delve too deep and risk deflowering her. That would come later, when they married. As they would, now that he had resolved to speak to Papa.

Then all thought got lost as her orgasm held her on the edge of the chasm and chased any further sensibility into the mists of bliss. Every out breath brought a whimper, and all she knew was his smell, his taste, and his touch as she writhed and bucked beneath him. Sweat slicked her panting body while hot moisture coated her thighs, and heat and tension gripped her core.

She came, trembling and crying his name. He held her and kept his fingers busy until she stilled and relaxed beneath him. It took a while for the waves of ecstasy to work through her, leaving her limp and spent. Then she became aware that his erection continued to nudge against her bared thigh and lax fingers. She whispered in his ear, 'What about you?'

'I'll take care of it later; I don't want to risk soiling your beautiful dress.' He sucked on his hand and groaned. 'I shall remember your taste and smell as I pleasure myself. My ears shall hear your cries while my hand brings me release.' When he fell silent, he placed a lingering kiss on her lips, one that now spoke of sweet love more than unbridled passion, and then eased his weight from her. 'We should get back, or they'll miss us.'

Although reluctant, Annalise nodded and eased into a seated position, where she set about putting herself back to rights while David did the same.

Before they left the arbour, David pulled her into his embrace for a final kiss, and then said, 'I'll come find you later. After I've spoken with your father.'

Unable to comprehend waiting until the morning for news, Annalise nodded. When he sent her back to the house ahead of him, a bereft ache settled into her chest and abdomen. How would she survive the next few hours without her love?

David hadn't yet sought her out, and it had grown late—too late for a young lady to wait up any longer. With a heavy heart and a dismayed sigh, Annalise allowed Betsy to undress her and ready her for bed. Once the maid had slipped the nightie over Annalise's head, she dismissed her, pleading exhaustion from the night's excitement. The maid left, and Annalise flopped onto her back, atop the folded down covers, and stared at the shadows the candle sent frolicking across the ceiling. What had become of her love? What had Papa decided? Worry gnawed at her lungs while she worried her bottom lip.

The candle burned low, and a chill slid over her. Resigned to having to wait until morning, Annalise slipped beneath the heavy blankets, snuffed the candle, and curled up on her side. Tiredness dragged at her eyelids, and soon, she fell into a doze.

Something in the room changed, and Annalise roused. Behind weak candlelight, stood a figure in silhouette. She rose to a sitting position and stared. His smell drifted to her … musky and all male. David … she would know his scent anywhere. He stepped closer, a finger to his lips.

The mattress dipped beneath his weight when he sat next to her. Annalise sought his eyes, and the sadness there undid her. With a sob, she gripped his arm just above the elbow. 'Oh, my love,' she murmured.

David set the candle onto the nightstand, and then turned to her and took hold of both her hands. Annalise held her breath, desperate to hear his news, while he sighed and leaned his forehead against hers. When he spoke, it came in a whisper, but carried ferocity for all that.

'Damn him. I have been denied, in no uncertain terms. They

are sending me away. I am to leave at first light, for London. Apologies for the impropriety of coming to your chambers like this, but I couldn't bear the thought of leaving without seeing you one last time.'

Robbed of words, Annalise wrapped her arms around his shoulders and pulled him into a tight embrace. Her tears dampened his warm neck. After a sniffle, she asked, 'Is there nothing to be done?'

He shook his head, then brushed his lips to her tears—first one cheek, then the other. 'We could run away, but I have neither my inheritance nor my profession. My studies are not yet complete, and will take another year. Ma'ma would have no hesitation in disinheriting me, and your father none in cutting off my allowance. We would be penniless.' He paused, deep in thought, then turned haunted eyes to her. 'If only we had another year …'

Annalise brightened. 'I could delay. If outright refusal fails, then I shall ensure a long engagement. What do you think?'

David nuzzled her lips, then said, 'It could work. It has to be worth a shot. Good girl.' He kissed her, and she parted for him. His tongue found hers and wrapped around it. With a moan of pleasure, she ran her fingers through his hair and pulled his head closer. He delved deeper into her mouth, as though he couldn't get in far enough, and then thrust his tongue in and out in a manner that reminded her of his caressing fingers in the arbour.

Slick wetness coated her between her legs. What would it be like if he used his tongue on her *down there*? A shudder rippled through her at the thought, and her cheeks flushed—half shamed, fully aroused. David eased back and studied her. 'What is it, my love? Did I hurt you?'

She shook her head. 'No.'

Concern oozed from him. 'I've offended you. My heart, I hadn't intended to lay hands on your person—'

She cut him off with her lips on his, then said, 'I trust you, and know you would never do anything to cause me embarrassment or harm.'

A perplexed frown crossed his face. 'Then what, my love?

Please, tell me. I cannot bear to part from you on such terms.'

Annalise flushed further. 'I-I was just remembering … t-tonight. How nice …'

He raised her hand to his mouth and kissed her knuckles, while staring into her eyes. 'I should never have done that. Should never have taken such liberties.'

Annalise set her jaw in determination. 'If we are to be parted, then I want to know as much of you as I can before you go. Propriety be damned.'

'Oh, my love, you know not what you say.'

'Well, I'm glad. Even now, I crave your touch.' Proud eyes dared him to sensor her.

David shook his head and made to stand, but Annalise pulled him back down to her and kissed him thoroughly. 'Touch me, like before. I beg of you, don't leave me like this.'

For reply, he pushed her down so that she lay on her back, and then he covered her with his body, exploring her with his lips and tongue the whole time. He tried one last time to curtail their passion, 'Annalise, I cannot promise restraint this time.'

Shocked at her audacious forwardness, she grabbed his hardness through his nightshirt. 'Ah, fuck.' His hips bucked, and he hissed through his teeth, then plunged his tongue into her mouth again. Without his earlier gentleness or control, he grabbed her breast through her nightie and squeezed. His knee nudged her legs apart, and she opened them wide for him. He knelt between her thighs and eased her nightie up. When he got to her thighs, she lifted her hips so that he could tug it up further. Then she lifted her torso to allow him to divest her of the garment entirely. As soon as he'd pulled it from over her head, she lay back on the bed and gazed up at him with passion-filled eyes.

His erection made a tent of his nightshirt. Mischief and desire deepened her voice when she said, 'Your turn.'

He ripped off his covering in one move, and she gasped at the sight of him kneeling between her legs, naked, and fully aroused. Teeth nibbling at her lower lip, Annalise reached out a hand and stroked him. He growled low in his throat, then stayed her hand. 'I won't last long if you do that. I'm still reeling from the arbour.' He grinned. Then he reached down and dipped a finger between her wet folds and entered her. She gasped and arched her back, pushing him into her further. Her nipples pebbled and throbbed as he plunged in and out of her. Then he withdrew, and Annalise whimpered.

Eyes locked on hers, he slipped his finger into his mouth and sucked her juice. 'Mmm. I've never supped anything so fine.'

Hesitant, a little afraid, and a lot aroused, Annalise asked, 'Can you … can you k-kiss me, down there?'

David's eyes widened, then a slow smile crept onto his face. Silent, he lowered his head between her legs and pushed her knees until her thighs parted fully for him. Then he pulled a leg over his shoulder and licked at her entrance. Beneath him, Annalise bucked and writhed, and a soft moan of utter pleasure slid from her. Then he plunged his tongue into her. Annalise shoved a fist into her mouth to muffle her cries. Never had she felt anything like this.

He lapped at her wetness with moans of appreciation. Delirious with desire, Annalise gripped his hair and held his head in place. He fucked her with his tongue, and circled her clit with his fingers. He slid a thumb through her slick folds, coating it in her fluid, and then teased her back entrance with it. David repeated the motion a few times, until both his thumb and her back passage grew slick with her juices, and then he pushed his thumb into her.

Heaven came down to Earth, and stars burst behind her eyelids. 'David!' she cried as she came. Annalise came and came and came. He continued to fuck her with his tongue, and thrust in and out of her with his thumb at her other entrance, and the waves of her orgasm rolled through her, on and on. Until, at last, she collapsed, utterly spent, back to the bed.

David eased out of her and kissed his way up her body until he reached her breasts. He sucked first one nipple, then the other into his mouth. Then he drifted up along her collarbone and nuzzled her neck. When his lips met hers, she could taste herself on his tongue. While a little off-putting, she also found it incredibly erotic. Tongue dancing with hers, he worked his hot, hard shaft along the wet channel of her folds, and the noise of her wetness reached her ears.

Annalise moaned into his mouth, and he reached behind her and fondled her buttocks, pressing himself closer to her. Need coursed through her, and despite her orgasm, she felt a deep ache of longing low down. A deep, instinctual urge to have him thrust inside her took her in its grasp until, panting, she begged him, 'Please. Oh, please.'

Her murmured pleas slipped into his mouth, and his return moan sent arrows of arousal straight to her core. Annalise lifted her hips to meet his, and the head of his cock nudged at her slick entrance. With a hand, he eased himself into position. Eyes holding hers, he thrust into her.

Annalise gasped at the sudden pain, and he stilled, watching her. Then his lips crushed hers and his tongue pushed into her mouth once more. He remained still inside her, stretching her and filling her, giving her time to adjust to his girth within. The pain reduced to a slight sting, and passion moved Annalise's hips beneath him. Slow and careful, he slipped out of her, and then pushed in again. At this gentle pace, he made love to her, and Annalise wrapped her legs around his waist and rocked with him.

The tempo built, and soon he thrust hard and fast, grunting each time his balls slapped at her, and the head of his cock hit a spot deep within her core that had her clawing at his back and crying out. She bit down on his shoulder to muffle her uncontrollable whimpers and moans. David increased the speed even more, and waves of ecstasy crashed through her. Annalise came again, and it seemed a hundred times more powerful than the release he'd given her with his tongue.

The orgasm broke her rhythm beneath him, and she buried her head into his neck. David thrust even harder and faster, and then a loud grunt broke from him as he stilled within her, groin tight against hers. Hot heat filled her, and she could feel him pulsing against her tight, wet walls. Then he collapsed against her and nuzzled at her neck.

Spent, he slipped from her and eased his weight to the side. The smell of their sex drifted up to her. David leaned down and kissed her, long and slow. 'Oh, my love.'

They lay entangled for some while, until neither of them could no longer deny that he must make a move soon if he were to avoid discovery by the soon-to-be-rousing household. He left her with kisses and promises to come back for her soon. When the door closed behind him, Annalise rolled to her side and sobbed into her pillows, heartbroken.

In disgrace for even thinking about having affections for her stepbrother, Annalise sat at breakfast alone in her room. Which suited her just fine. What didn't suit nearly so well, was the look Betsy had given her upon entering her room and awakening her. The two women shared a whole book in that one glance. Grim-faced, the maid flung the windows open wide to admit fresh air, and then stripped the bed-linens. Then she had staff fetch hot water for a bath, and set about giving Annalise a thorough scrubbing.

Afterward, pink faced from the heat and vigorous rubs, Annalise took herself for a walk in the gardens. Agitation and fretting rendered her incapable of occupying herself seated in the parlour. Upon her return to the house, a nasty surprise awaited her. After sending David packing, Papa had invited Mr Jones to join them for an indefinite period.

Deaf to her pleas, her parents moved along the enforced courtship. When Annalise challenged her stepmother about the situation, the woman explained a few facts of which the girl had been in ignorance. Papa had squandered the family fortune. All that remained was their good name. Mr Jones represented financial stability, if not love, and—in return—marriage into the Cheviots assured him the social connexions that he lacked as 'new money'.

If Annalise refused the liaison, she would condemn her family—her *whole* family—to destitution and social exile. She couldn't do that to David. If for no one else's sake, she had to do it for him. Then, her monthly failed to arrive with its customary punctuality. Annalise confided in Betsy, who'd already proven her trustworthiness—disapproval notwithstanding—who confirmed her worst fears.

In a panic, unable to see any other avenue, Annalise finally acquiesced and meekly consented to a date being set. Immediately, the indefatigable wheels of a society wedding set into motion. Announcements were made. Invitations sent out. And the few weeks passed in a flash. Annalise didn't understand Alfred's hurry, but it served her purposes.

Upon their union, Alfred received a peerage, and they became The Lord and Lady Alfred Jones of Pencarrow Manor. Society didn't stop there in its stripping away of her identity, but rolled right over any illusions of free will too. While Mr Jones had remained aloof and dispassionate during their 'courtship', he brought to bear an entirely different demeanour on their wedding night.

Not giving her any chance to approach the situation delicately, nor in a manner timely enough for her to acclimatise, he strode into her chamber from the adjoining shared dressing room, ripped her nightgown down the entire length of its front, and manhandled her roughly onto the bed, his erection bobbing disgustingly in front of him. Unlike David, body hair covered Alfred from head to toe. While his door-knocker beard struck Annalise as mildly absurd, his yeti-like back and chest filled her with loathing.

It seemed that foreplay hadn't made it into his repertoire, for he forced her legs apart and pounced. His entry rough and greedy. It hurt far more than losing her flower had; so much so that this felt more like her first time. Afraid, outraged, humiliated, squished, and in pain, Annalise lay beneath him stiff as a board and unyielding. He got on with it without her, and in a few quick thrusts, spilled his seed inside her.

With a grunt, he climbed from her and wiped himself on his nightshirt. Still without uttering a word, he left her laying there, sobs wracking her small body. Mercifully, she'd been allowed to keep Betsy, who now crept in with the vial of pig's blood held in her clenched fist. Annalise wiped her tears away and attempted to calm herself. Hopefully, the ignoramus wouldn't cotton that no blood marred his nightshirt where he'd cleaned himself. If her luck held, he would take confirmation from the blood-stained bedding that his manservant would confirm for him, come the morrow.

Had she believed things couldn't get worse? He took her by force every night for the next two weeks, until—at long last—he returned to London. The rest of the time, she may as well have not existed. It seemed that she wasn't the only one un-enamoured of their pairing. This, she could have borne, but not his publicly establishing his mistress at his dwelling in Chelsea. And, worse still, the disease he brought back to her upon his return.

The first sign came when an unpleasant and itchy rash appeared in her most private place. Mortified, she did her best to deal with it alone. Then came the miscarriage, and the doctor. Of course, as soon as he examined her, and listened to her many symptoms, he diagnosed Syphilitic infection. The doctor set her on a course of mercury treatments, and cautioned her to rest and recuperate. An hour after he left, Alfred came to her room.

Undeterred by her condition, sharing it himself, he tried to bed her. When she refused him, and yelled at him for doing this to her, he beat her black and blue. If not for Betsy running in at her screams, he would have taken her. However, the presence of others seemed to bring the beast to his senses, and he slammed out of her chamber and headed for his quarters.

The doctor returned the next day, and didn't try to hide his fury upon discovering Annalise's state. Gentle and attentive with her, he ordered an ambulance to convey her to the Bodmin hospital. Then he turned his wrath upon Lord Jones.

Dr Richmond came from an old and well respected line, and used all of his social clout to secure protection for Annalise. Later, seated by her bedside, he conveyed to her his actions to reassure her of her altered position. The doctor had threatened Alfred with public exposure if he failed to leave her alone from there on in. Alfred would reside in his London Chelsea dwelling, along with his mistress, and provide Annalise with an allowance. Furthermore, he would provide her with accommodations for those times she may wish to travel to

London. Should Lord Jones wish to make use of his estate, he would do so without verbal (or other) intercourse with his wife, and his mistress would remain in London.

Divorce being out of the question without bringing great shame, this seemed the best outcome she could have hoped for. Of course, society was all about keeping face. Unfortunately, she reacted badly to the mercury and had to cease treatment. The syphilis progressed, and left Annalise with a disfigured and grossly enlarged nose. The doctor did what he could, but the malady left her with a hole where her nostrils and septum would have been.

Annalise became a recluse, and had long since given up any hope of ever seeing David again. Despite the separation, she remained a married woman, and who in their right mind would consort with her in her current physical state? Even wearing the apparatus to cover her nose, and reduce the pain the exposure to bright light brought, she couldn't escape the fact of her infectious disease.

Years passed in this way, and then Dr Richmond paid an unexpected visit. A new treatment was being trialled in London. He urged her to give the matter some thought. 'The Salvarsan is much more efficacious than the mercury, and it carries far less risk. Please, my dear, think about it.'

⚜

Distraught, Dr David Waverley braced his elbows on the desktop and put his head in his hands. Upon hearing of Annalise's marriage to some banker from the City, he had given her up. She had failed to wait for him, and he couldn't bear to be in her company if she couldn't be his. Nor did he wish to learn anything of her marriage partner.

And so, bitter, he had stayed away. Had completed his studies, and now held a consultant position at the Samuelson Hospital on Grosvenor Street. The high level of surgical competition between the many London hospitals worked in his favour—hence his rapid rise to a senior position.

'I had no idea.' He looked at her, cheeks pale and jaw

trembling. 'Why did you not seek me out sooner? I would have given you every assistance.' He rubbed at his eyes. 'I believed you'd changed your mind and had forgotten me.'

Annalise smiled, but a stray tear slipped beneath her glasses and betrayed her. 'Oh, David. I'm not the young girl you fell in love with. Somewhere along the way, a squall swept her over a cliff and dashed her lifeless soul on the jagged rocks below. For a long time, I believed there was no coming back from that. Fatal the injury may not have been, but enough to disfigure and destroy. And it seemed that the damned surf just kept pounding, relentless in its assault. How could I bring such a storm to you?' A dainty hand reached up and wiped away a further tear. 'I learned all I could of you. It filled me with pride to hear how you had succeeded. Even now, I come here against my better judgement, but Dr Richmond holds great powers of persuasion. And he had a point; I've already lost face, and here is a chance to save it.'

David, decision made, leapt to his feet and strode around the table. By her side, he crouched and took hold of her hands. 'I can help you. Right here, at this hospital, we are working with this new drug. And, I am certain, we can perform surgery to restore you. Recovery will be long and painful, but it will work. That I promise you.'

'Why? With all that I have done?'

'I never ceased my affections, Annalise. And, I see now, that nor did you. In fact, fault has to lie with me as well. I never should have taken you the way I did. It put you at great peril, and only by the grace of God—'

'And the love of Betsy.' Her smile brightened the room.

David chuckled. 'Yes, by the love of Betsy, too. What if your husband had discovered your subterfuge? From what I've heard, I could well imagine that he would have killed you.'

Her small frame shuddered, and she gripped his hands tighter.

David pleaded with his eyes. 'You came here in search of my help, and now I beg of you to allow me to give it. I can be discreet.'

'Yes.' One word. Small and quiet. Enough to move

mountains.

David scheduled the surgery for the following week. While the procedure took a matter of hours, the recovery needed weeks. He had made a skin flap on her upper arm and grafted this to just above what remained of her nose. The flap had to remain attached to her arm until the graft took and her body grew a blood supply to it. He couldn't imagine the pain and discomfort from having an arm strapped up in such a position for such a long time, but his dear Annalise remained stoic and never uttered a complaint in his presence.

He visited daily, and when his schedule allowed, twice a day. After the first week, and once assured of her eventual recovery, David had her moved to a care home halfway between Samuel's and her apartments by Regents Park.

Today, finally, saw the time arrive for her to undertake her last surgery. This would disengage the flap from her arm and see he and his team of surgeons craft her a new nose. The fix would never replace the bone she'd lost, but it would look a darn sight better than the awful hole she bore at the moment. And, after the scar tissue had healed, the repair could be passed off as being from an injury instead of being the obvious Syphilitic curse it was.

The surgery went well, and a week later, David had her released into his care. He arranged to have her belongings and her person taken to his home in Westminster. Months of recuperation still lay ahead, and he intended to spend every moment he could in her company.

While Annalise's long confinement drew to a close, mixed feelings frothed and bubbled within David's veins. On the one hand, her recovery exceeded all expectations, and to see her with only a minimal of disfigurement and full use of her arm restored, filled him with joy. On the other, this could only mean that she would leave him soon. As convalescent and physician, society afforded them limited leeway. However, her return to health and vitality demanded that this married Lady quit her quarters in the home of this bachelor—stepbrother notwithstanding. Especially as she worried that Lord Jones may yet make trouble for them.

Her complicated marital situation also prevented Annalise from being open to any rekindling between them. Which proved just as well, because the good Lord Jones did, indeed, attempt to slur her character. Their proper behaviour, and witnesses aplenty to back that up, resulted in him driving away in such a fury that he kicked up gravel from the short drive when he sped away in his new motorcar. Had David been home for Lord Jones' visit, he would likely have pummelled the man to a pulp. Perhaps just as well that he'd been delayed in a surgery. As it was, rage and disgust had struck him when his staff recounted events to him.

David rushed to Annalise's side in the parlour, but she sat there calm—if a little withdrawn. 'I've made arrangements to open my apartments at Regents. Betsy assures me that I may return by week's end.'

The doctor could only nod, pensive. The fire roared and flickered in the grate, and the dancing flames drew his gaze. Dare he suggest divorce? Had he not brought her enough shame? Even though only three people held the secret of their tryst, Annalise bore the burden within her heart. He could not, in all conscience, add to its weight. Meantime, neither of them remained so young or carefree as they had been those few years ago. Damn it, though, her reacquaintance had rendered him entirely incapable of seeking solace elsewhere, no matter his growing frustration.

Dr Richmond and his fair wife, Leanna, arrived and joined them, and the party moved to the drawing room. Shortly after, the bell rang for dinner and brought a welcome distraction from David's dark thoughts. He took Annalise's arm and escorted her to the dining room. Leanna engaged Annalise in lively conversation, and David made great effort to afford the good doctor his attention.

Half an hour into the main course, hooves clattered outside, and then came frantic pounding at the front door. Even while his manservant made haste to answer it, David rose to his feet, expecting some urgent summons or other from Samuel's. The messenger, however, came not for him but for Annalise. Apparently, the good Lord Alfred Jones had lost control of his shiny new motorcar and careened from the road en route to his country estate. He now lay in critical condition at the county hospital, and Lady Alfred Jones must attend him as soon as possible.

Dr and Mrs Richmond offered their assistance, and arranged to travel with Lady Jones to see her safely to Pencarrow manor, and then onward to Bodmin. David cursed that he had obligations here in the city that he couldn't possibly wriggle out of. Within the hour, a carriage and four whisked his love away.

The next few days saw David sending Annalise's belongings on, as she would not be returning to his abode come what may. Betsy liaised with him and the remaining staff to ensure that Annalise's Regents Park apartments were closed down once more and anything she needed packed up ready for transportation to the manor.

After this whirlwind few months, David found himself more alone and desolate than he had been before she'd turned up at his office that day. It had felt easier to believe that she no longer held him in her esteem. To know her situation, and her feelings, left him frustrated and angry. He lasted as long as he could, and then decided that they could all be damned for all he cared. Surely, as her brother, he could now take leave from work and pay his sister a visit?

David made his arrangements and took a train to Plymouth, where he had a fast coach take him on to Pencarrow. The butler greeted him upon his arrival, and showed him to his rooms, while informing him that her Ladyship had received grave news from Bodmin just that morning and had returned to the hospital. She'd left instructions that David should be offered every courtesy and given the freedom of the house and estate in her absence. It took every ounce of self-control not to go to her. Instead, he saddled up and took the stable lad's suggestion of a pleasant ride through the hill-valley to the Camel. Apparently, her Ladyship often enjoyed riding the route whenever at home.

At the river, he led the horse to the bank for a drink, and then tethered it to a nearby branch. Then he returned to the river's edge and scooped up water with which he splashed his face.

The sun bathed him in warmth, and he stripped down to his breeches and shirtsleeves, then lay in the grass. In spite of his agitation, he fell into a doze in the early afternoon heat. The neighing of his horse, followed by the dull thud of an approaching rider, roused him.

David opened his eyes and squinted into the bright glare. A lady. Horseback. Hurriedly, he rose to his feet. Before he could dress himself properly, she came upon him. He stood and stared as Annalise leapt from the saddle, ran to him, and threw her arms around his neck. A stranger may think that her bright smile conflicted with her exclamation, 'He's dead.' However, David knew better. Knew the relief that must bring her.

He pulled her into his arms and lifted her from the ground. Then, returning her feet to the soil, he planted a kiss on her forehead. Annalise stepped back from his arms and gazed up at him. 'It's so good to see you. And now … soon … we'll be … I'm free, David. If you'll have me?'

His next kiss found eager lips, and soon his tongue mated with hers while his hands squeezed her pliant buttocks through her riding skirt. Even through the fabric, her heat caressed his hard length. David eased to his knees and pulled her with him.

Annalise giggled and wriggled out of his grasp. 'Well? Will you have me?'

David grinned. 'Oh. I intend to have you, all right.' Then he claimed her mouth with his. Her outraged giggle sent vibrations straight from his tongue to his cock, which twitched in his pants. He ground his hips into her with a groan. 'Tell me you don't intend to make me wait,' he murmured into her neck.

'A long time.' Her hot breath tickled his ear. This time, his cock didn't twitch, it leapt. 'I have to observe months of mourning and—'

He cut off her teasing with his lips and tongue. Then he moved to her neck, where he nuzzled and suckled. Annalise bucked in his arms and threw her head back. David dropped her onto the ground and rose to his feet, mischief lighting his eyes. 'Well, then, I'll have to find my satisfaction elsewhere.'

'You wouldn't dare!'

God but her indignation was damn sexy.

'Perhaps a lady could use her powers of persuasion …'

Contagious fiend that it was, the mischief jumped from his eyes to hers. The little vixen used her pale blue orbs to hold his gaze captive while her hands made slow, tantalising work of unfastening her blouse and easing it open. Her flushed breasts pushed against her brassiere and her chest heaved. 'Persuade you? No, I don't think so.' She licked her full, red lips.

'No?' He dropped to his knees at her side and slid a hand into the cleft between her sweet mounds. 'Keep on not persuading me, will you?'

With another giggle, she told him, 'Your wish is my command.' Then she pulled him on top of her.

The hard bulge in his breeches pressed into the Y at the junction of her thighs, and she wriggled beneath him. Then her fingers got to work on his shirt buttons, and soon they lay skin-to-skin from the waist up. Except for her bra. David slipped the straps down her shoulders and onto her arms, then eased her nipples free. As he reached beneath her spine, seeking the clasp, he nipped at her erect buds with his teeth. Then he lathed at them with his tongue. The hooks came free, and he slipped the troublesome garment from her.

A glance at her face revealed desire in her dilated pupils and flushed cheeks. David nipped and sucked his way over her breasts, along the delicate collarbone, and up her neck, until he settled on her luscious mouth. She smelled of lavender and honey, and tasted just as sweet. A light sheen covered her skin, and he lapped at its alluring saltiness. Her dainty little tongue flicked around his, and she scraped his back with her nails.

'Oh, David.'

'Tell me what you want me to do to you.'

A gasp escaped her parted lips, and she hesitated, but then said, 'Touch me. With your hands and mouth. Taste every inch of my flesh. I've missed the feel of your tongue inside me.'

Another gasp saw her lips claiming his and her tongue invading his mouth.

Her words brought his arousal to new heights. In a tangle of lips, tongues, and limbs, he wrestled her skirt from her, and then rid her of her undergarments. The sun shone down on her naked glory, as she lay on her back, legs spread wide for him. Moisture glistened on her folds and dampened her pubic hair.

David delayed long enough to shuck out of his breeches and underwear, and then plunged his head between her thighs. Annalise moaned and writhed beneath him while he licked and sucked, and finally fucked her with his tongue. The taste and smell of her sex drove him wild, as did her moans and whimpers. Never could he tire of his sweet Annalise.

A rush of juices over his mouth and tongue gave him his long-awaited taste of her ejaculation while her orgasm shuddered through her. She bucked and gripped him between her thighs, riding his face, and he continued to penetrate with his tongue and fingers until she settled beneath him, a satisfied sigh purring out of her.

David moved up her body until his mouth found hers. She kissed him passionately, and wrapped her small, hot hand around his shaft. Fisted around him, she stroked down his length, pulling his foreskin back, and brushed her thumb over the moist slit in the head of his cock. He groaned and rocked his groin. Their teeth clacked gently as he attacked her mouth anew.

And then she rolled so that he lay on his back. Annalise rested on hands and knees above him and licked her lips. Then she dipped her head and licked him. 'Ah, fuck.' He gasped and fisted handfuls of grass, trying to hold onto control for a little longer. He nearly lost it when she sucked him into her hot, wet little mouth and lathed him with her naughty tongue.

While she sucked on his hard length, which stretched her lips around it, she worked him up and down with her hand. Every now and then, she made little grunting noises, which sent vibrations down his cock and straight into his balls. His lower abdomen clenched tight, and his sac rose up into his groin—tight and ready. He wouldn't last much longer, and tried to warn her, 'I'm going to explode at any second.'

For reply, she increased her pace and pressure. With the next lap of her tongue over the head, he came hard. His seed burst into her mouth, and he gave a gruff bark while he bucked into her face. She continued to lick and swallow until she'd taken everything he'd given. Only when he began to soften did she rise and slide up his body. She wrapped her legs around his, and her wetness coated his thigh.

David pulled her into a cuddle and nibbled at her lips, while pressing kisses to her cheeks, chin, and forehead. Although her surgery had healed well and looked good, he felt wary of risking any pain by kissing her nose. As if she'd read his mind, she looked up at him and said, 'It's okay. You can kiss me there, if you want. I remember how you used to love pecking me on the nose.' Her smile and invitation reassured him, and he pressed a tentative kiss to the grafted tissue. Then he returned to her mouth, and finally, pulled her head into his chest. He breathed deep through his nose and took in the scent of her while he held her close.

They lay together, naked in the grass, until the sun dipped lower and a cold breeze heralded the oncoming intrusion of evening, and perhaps a summer shower. Lazily, David dressed Annalise before tending to himself. Curious, roaming hands and lips kept hindering his efforts, but they got there in the end. They rode in companionable silence, side by side, back to Pencarrow Manor, where—perforce—they had to part, even if only temporarily.

To maintain decorum through dinner almost killed him, but the household staff stole any chance of play. The two of them discussed what the future may bring, and Annalise fretted about what surprises Alfred's will may hold. David well knew how little they could influence anything, and so diverted her with anecdotes from his years in the profession and some of the antics his juniors and trainees had gotten up to. Besides, he would inherit soon enough, and Alfred's investment assistance had given the Cheviot-Waverley estate the boost it had so desperately needed.

Later that night, and every night thereafter, once the staff had bedded down, David snuck to Annalise's room. He took her in every position he knew, and together they learned yet more. She proved an adventurous woman, generous with her loving. Despite the excitement of experimentation, nothing could beat staring into her eyes while she lay on her back and he slid in and out of her hot, wet core. Nor could any sound ever compare to that of her crying his name while she trembled and writhed beneath him, lost in the throes of passion.

The will settled—absent any shocks—and the proper period of mourning observed, David decided to make things official. Already, he'd secured a position as surgeon at Bodmin, with the help of Dr Richmond, who had grown into a firm and valued friend. And David's new motorcar would make the journey between the hospital and Pencarrow much shorter than it would have been via horse and coach. Perhaps innovation wasn't so overrated after all. Summer had given way to autumn, and the days had grown too cold to take Annalise down by the river where they had reconnected, so he grabbed her in the stable one day. None of the hands were around, and David snatched his opportunity. Improvisation was one of the most important tools of his trade, and he put his imagination to full use now.

Amidst her giggles and the snorting of the horses, he pleasured her with his tongue and hands. Two loud orgasms later, he gave her a thorough fucking. Then, as she lay panting and satiated beneath him, he rolled to his side and propped himself up on his elbow.

'My sweet, dearest Annalise, you are my heart, my soul, my everything.'

She giggled, and he shushed her with a gentle finger to her lips.

He tried again, 'My sweet, dearest Annalise, you are my heart, my soul, my everything. You give me breath, heart, and life. I would be the happiest man there's ever been, if you would consent to be my wife.'

She stopped breathing. Actually stopped. His heart paused

with her. And then she squealed and threw her arms around David's neck. 'Yes. Oh yes. Forever and always.'

It took a bit of fumbling through the hay and discarded clothes, but at last, he found the little box and retrieved the ring. And really, this slight downside to proposing naked paled in light of the many bonuses. The modest diamond glinted in the rays of the low winter sun that found its way into the stable. David slipped the gold band onto her finger and leaned down for a kiss. His cock celebrated by rising to the occasion, and prodded her in the hip as he claimed her mouth. Utter joy spilled from him as he claimed his love.

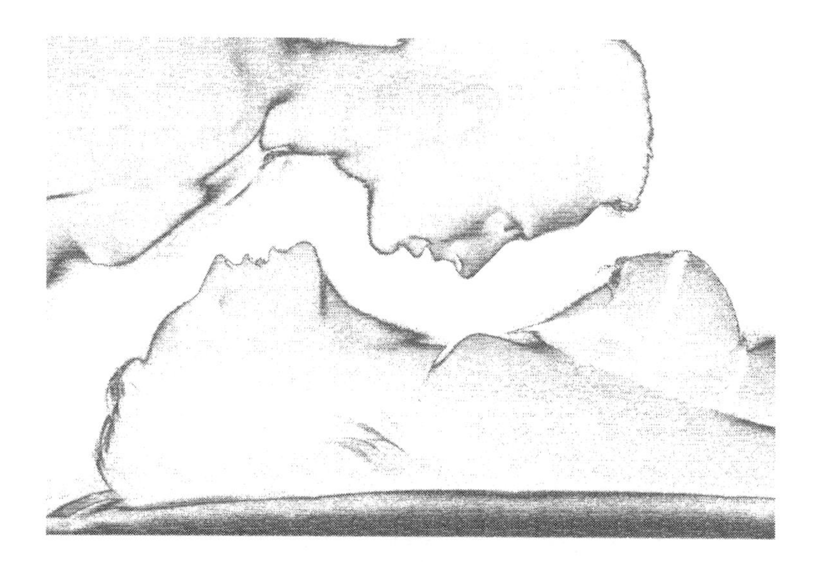

More Books from Harmony

Non-fiction
Polish Your Prose: Essential Editing Tips for Authors

Young Adult Fiction
Elemental Earth: Book One in the Mysteries series

Fantasy Fiction
The Battle for Brisingamen

Mystery/Thriller
The Glade

Women's Fiction
Finding Katie

Poetry
Slices of Soul

Erotic Fiction
Interludes

Anthologies
Rave Soup for the Writer's Soul Vol 1
Rave Soup for the Writer's Soul Vol 2
All Authors Anthology: Unity
All Authors Anthology: Vitality

Find all these books on the author's Amazon Author Page at: http://www.amazon.com/Harmony-Kent/e/B00CO0AR7U/ref=dp_byline_cont_pop_ebooks_1

Printed in Poland
by Amazon Fulfillment
Poland Sp. z o.o., Wrocław